Even Cowgirls Get the Blues

John— you have a great writing talent— I hope this book helps you develop even more— I thought of you when I read it—

Love, K

CELEBRITIES AND CIVILIANS TELL STORIES OF THE BEST LOST, TOSSED, AND FOUND ITEMS FROM AROUND THE WORLD

Requiem for a Paper Bag

edited by Davy Rothbart

A FIRESIDE BOOK
Published by Simon & Schuster
New York   London   Toronto   Sydney

Fireside
A Division of Simon & Schuster, Inc.
1230 Avenue of the Americas
New York, NY 10020

First Fireside trade paperback edition May 2009

FIRESIDE and colophon are registered trademarks of Simon & Schuster, Inc.

For information about special discounts for bulk purchases, please contact Simon & Schuster Special Sales at 1-800-456-6798 or business@simonandschuster.com

The Simon & Schuster Speakers Bureau can bring authors to your live event. For more information or to book an event contact the Simon & Schuster Speakers Bureau at 1-866-248-3049 or visit our website at www.simonspeakers.com.

Designed by Richard Oriolo

Illustrations by Dan Tice, Ghostshrimp, Brendt Rioux, and Ben Snakepit

Cover design by Michael Wartella

Manufactured in the United States of America

10 9 8 7 6 5 4 3 2 1

Library of Congress Cataloging-in-Publication Data
    Requiem for a paper bag : celebrities and civilians tell stories of the best lost, tossed, and found items from around the world / edited by Davy Rothbart.
        p. cm.
      "A Fireside book."
      1. Lost articles—Catalog. I. Rothbart, Davy. II. Found magazine.
    AM501.L67R47 2009
    081—dc22   2009006660
ISBN-13: 978-1-4165-6054-8
ISBN-10:   1-4165-6054-8

CONTENTS

HI THERE! WELCOME. THIS IS THE INTRODUCTION.

Whenever I'm on a plane and the person sitting next to me asks what I do for a living, I always get a bit nervous. How do I explain to a stranger that I spend my days looking through scraps of paper that other people have found on the ground and mailed to me—which means, essentially, that I examine trash? What's striking, though, is that once I've muddled through an explanation, my row mate always gets excited and shares a story with me about a bizarre photo or message in a bottle that they once discovered. I swear, this happens every single time. Young or old, rich or poor, country folk or city folk—apparently, the appeal of finding interesting shit is universal.

For the past several years, as my brother Peter and I have zoomed around the country putting on our *FOUND Magazine* shows, I've been lucky enough to hear hundreds of stories from people about cool stuff that they've found, ranging from the kind of personal notes and letters we publish in the magazine to things that would be difficult to publish, like mummies, or exotic frogs. What would happen, I wondered, if I asked my favorite writers, musicians, filmmakers, and other awesome folks to reveal the stories of their own most memorable finds? The results—wildly funny, provocative, wrenching, and deeply weird—are collected in this book.

The assignment I gave was simple: Share a personal story about something fascinating that you yourself have found, or write a piece of fiction sparked by a particular find. As the stories rolled in, I couldn't help but be struck by two things—how vastly different each piece was and also how many resonances they had with one another. In every case, finding something had produced a sizable shift in the finder's life.

Jonathan Lethem and OK Go's Damian Kulash talk about tiny notes they found that continue to play big roles in their creative lives. Comedian Patton Oswalt and writer Kevin Dole 2 talk about finding wallets and their awkward efforts to return them, while PostSecret's Frank Warren, Scrabble champ Marlon Hill, and musician Billy Bragg discover the magic of rocks. Jesse Thorn, America's radio sweetheart, finds a magic tree bearing a fairy gun; *Saturday Night Live*'s Andy Samberg finds money—$5,000, to be exact; David Simon, creator of *The Wire*, finds hints of a missing Bob Dylan letter that could potentially be worth much more. Writer Susan Orlean finds a pitched newspaper that propels her into the adventure of her life, while Jenji Kohan, creator of *Weeds*, has her thrift-store adventures pruned short by the unexpected appearance of a bloody jockstrap. Eli Horowitz, managing editor of *McSweeney's*, finds a frog; musician Devendra Banhart finds a frog guarding a breathtaking photograph; and legendary Hollywood producer Robert Evans tries to keep a lobster in the picture during a special trip to Hawaii. Chuck D builds a car out of found materials; Jim Carroll finds a soldier in an unexpected place; and Michael Yon, reporting from Iraq, finds an unexpected letter on a terrorist's laptop. One thing I really love, in reading these pieces, is learning that I'm not the only one to ascribe special meaning and power to something that I've found. Andrew Bird finds a dope hat; Paulo Coelho finds a feather to put in it; and Seth Rogen is tickled pink after a precious discovery.

For a lot of writers, certain found notes and pictures themselves proved tantalizing enough to spark the idea for a story. Charles Baxter writes of a menacing note found blowing in a parking lot, and Steve Almond imagines a forbidden attraction from a photo of friends sipping beers in the back of a truck. A Kalashnikov bullet, meanwhile, drops from the sky and provides Mohsin Hamid with something to brag about when he gets to college and also the seed of his first novel.

Dozens of other lush and luscious found tales dot the landscape within, each one speaking to the mystery, the sense of wonder, and the unabashed thrill of finding something on the ground or on the street. The world is a magical place, and its magic expresses itself most exquisitely in the treasures it coughs up onto its gutters and curbs. Please enjoy all the found stories here, and please share your own found stories with us, as well as your finds—write to us, e-mail, call, or join us for a drink when we roll to your town!

Peace out for now—DAVY

A TREE GROWS IN VANCOUVER: PART I

Seth Rogen

Seth Rogen is a writer, actor, film producer, and comedian. His movies include *Knocked Up*, *Superbad*, and *Pineapple Express*.

I was eleven years old. Sure, I'd seen a *Playboy* before, and even *Playboy* had blown my mind. But I'd never seen anything hard-core—to any degree—before this particular day.

For some strange reason, my mom had signed me up to do a play in Chinatown, and I'd arrived early to the rehearsal. While I was waiting, I decided to take a little stroll around the Sun Yat-Sen Gardens, which is this amazing Asian garden in Vancouver—it's actually in a pretty dangerous neighborhood, but I didn't know that at eleven. So I was walking around, killing time, when I noticed a magazine lying mashed and crumpled on the ground. I moved closer and saw body parts—*naked* body parts. Holy shit! Even from one tiny glimpse, I could tell it was more explicit than anything I'd ever seen in my life.

I kept walking—I didn't even slow my pace. But when I reached the end of the block, something drew me back. I turned and walked by the magazine again, just to get one more glance. And then again. I began circling the thing like a shark—stealing little peeks at the pages on the ground. It had been raining all week so the magazine wasn't just crumpled, it was soaking wet, too. I walked by it a fourth time and then, trying to act casual, bent down and snatched it up. It was just a big wet sopping mess; I shoved the whole thing in my jacket pocket. I didn't look at it, just shoved it in there and went to my play rehearsal. Every ten or twenty minutes throughout the rehearsal, I sneaked over to my jacket to make sure that the hot, wet clump was still inside.

That night I went home and carefully spread the magazine on a towel to dry out. Then I stared. I couldn't believe what I was looking at. It all seemed much more surgical than I'd ever imagined it would be. I mean, I saw the insides of body parts I had never even seen the outsides of before. I was shocked at how explicit it was. "They're just *showing* people having sex!" At that age, sex is such an unattainable Holy Grail. To see it nonchalantly plastered all over this magazine was unbelievable to me. I used to look at these pages constantly. I don't even think I jacked off at that point—I would go to my room and just *stare*.

You may not believe this, but I still look at porno from time to time. As you know, they have ads toward the backs of porno magazines for phone-sex lines and shit like that. My original porno mag was so waterlogged that the ad pages in the back were, for the most part, the only ones undamaged enough to see. Well, I held on to that magazine for a very long time. Even after I got real porno—movies and whatnot—I still held on to that original find. I'm sure at some point my mom found the thing and threw it away. But believe me when I tell you this: There are actually the same *exact* ads in the backs of magazines today as the ones that were in that soggy porno magazine I found fifteen years ago. Trust me, I'm an expert.

A TREE GROWS IN VANCOUVER: PART II

Evan Goldberg

Evan Goldberg writes and produces comedy television and film. He also worked as an American Apparel model for three days in 2004.

My story is fantastically similar to Seth's, but with some key distinctions. I was not quite eleven—ten and a half, maybe. Okay, barely ten. Seth was in a part of town where you might've also found heroin and prostitutes, but I was in a nice part of town, walking around my neighborhood with my buddy Tim. Tim was an extremely intense Christian, very devout.

We were walking down the street when, lo and behold, sitting right there in front of us on the sidewalk was a porno mag. It was decidedly *not* wet. In fact, it had been raining every single day except for—miraculously—the previous two. The magazine wasn't hidden, it was just gleaming there in plain view, as if someone had said, "Let's put this here so that Evan can find it later." Tim, the devout Christian, was the one who grabbed it, and we quickly darted off to examine our new treasure.

Of course, once we were back in my room with the magazine, there was a big hullabaloo over what to do with it—we were completely freaked out at the prospect of our parents catching us with it. We were both kids with zero privacy. My mom was one of those mothers who didn't give me an inch; she was just *in there*. Tim's parents were profoundly religious and would've simply gone nuts if they knew he had porno.

So after much deliberation, we decided that the best possible solution was to hide the porno in a tree. Fortunately, we knew a particularly good tree. We ran down to the park a few streets over, scooted up the tree, and perched it on the highest branch. Unlike Seth, I'd been masturbating since I was eight, so before we left, I tore out a few pages to take home with me. Tim did, too. We agreed upon six pages each, with the idea that we'd ration our enjoyment of the magazine and that just a couple of pages would be more manageable to hide. Always thinking ahead, I took only advertisements, as those pages had the most pictures per page. I went home, folded the pages into a tiny cube the size of a pair of dice, and stashed it under the heaviest thing in my room, an enormous chest of drawers filled with cologne bottles given to me by an eccentric aunt.

In the week that followed, Tim and I would call each other every day: "Hey, you wanna go to the tree?" Sometimes I'd just go there on my own and he'd already be there, or vice versa. We'd make the long climb to the highest branch and uncover our hidden prize. I stared at that magazine forever; I would literally spend hours looking at one vagina. *Holy fuck*, I'd think, *that's a vagina, and I've seen all of it*. I felt that a vagina was something that could be solved.

But there was one thing we couldn't figure out: all the pictures of girls licking other girls' bums. What was up with that? For a long time I thought that girls licking girls' bums was a big deal. I was very confused. To make matters worse, I went to a rigid school primarily for kids from Hong Kong, and sex education there was a low priority. I'd go to Jewish summer camp and do my best to learn everything there was to learn about sex and then go back to a school where even kissing seemed dangerous.

Tim and I devoured that magazine in six-page bursts of pleasure. Eventually the reverse of what happened to Seth happened to me: It rained one fucking day. Of course, we'd been too stupid to put the magazine into a plastic bag, and it turned into pulpy mush. My heart was broken.

In many ways, I've experienced most of my momentous firsts as a sort of out-of body-experience. I'd had the same feeling when I'd found that porno as I'd had the moment when I first had sex, got my first blow job, and the first time I thought I was in love. You think to yourself, *I'm there! This is that moment! This is the moment where I become the guy who's had a blow job!* That's what it felt like to find that magazine on the curb—I was racing back to my house with Tim and at the same time thinking, *I've arrived at that time in my life where I get to see porno!* I was becoming, in a sense, a new me.

To this day, I still keep all my porn in that tree. Seth and I meet there, climb to the highest branch, and make out.

D. T.

JOEY RULES THE WORLD

Miranda July

Miranda July is a filmmaker, writer, and artist. She is the author of a book of stories, *No One Belongs Here More Than You*, and the film *Me and You and Everyone We Know*. She lives in Los Angeles.

When I was a kid, I used to religiously ask my dad if I could go through his trash. He'd grudgingly allow me to sift through his junk mail, old notes, lists, and abandoned, half-finished letters. His handwriting was eerie and intense, like a disturbed child's, but reading through his discarded papers gave me a sense of the tiny, strange details of his life, and it became a way to find intimacy with him. As I've grown up, my fascination with the bits and pieces of other people's lives has only increased. Out walking around, I'm the sort of person who always has to turn over each piece of paper I see to make sure the secrets of the universe aren't written on the other side.

At a Goodwill in Portland, Oregon, I found the diary of a high school girl who wanted desperately to be a good Christian, but was constantly drinking and having sex, then feeling guilty and repentant. Her little brother kept breaking into her diary and adding his own declarations. At one point he says: *JOEY RULES THE WORLD. HE HOLDS IT IN HIS HANDS*. Within all the heavy stuff on her mind, Joey busts in so full of life and so free of struggle. Then, on the next page, the girl simply continues on in her little bubbly handwriting; she makes no mention of her brother's trespasses or interjections, just goes back to her sorrowful tale.

Before I made my first movie, *Me and You and Everyone We Know*, I'd decided that in the last scene this guy would put a picture of flowers up in this tree. I needed just the right picture of flowers, so I went down the street from where I live to a place called the Millennium Thrift Store. This isn't your typical thrift store—it's basically a dumping ground for smelly garbage, filled with dirty, stained mattresses and lots of things you'd never ever want. They didn't have any pictures of flowers, but I saw one of a bird sitting in a tree and bought it for a quarter.

The guy at the register was trying to tell me in Spanish what kind of bird it was, but I was confused for a minute. Just as I was heading out the door, I realized that he was saying it was a quail. I smiled at him and for some reason tried to walk out of the store holding the picture the way a quail would. I remember thinking to myself, *Why am I doing this?* But then it struck me that something weird and interesting was happening—that this was a moment I needed to pay attention to. I'd call it a *found* moment. The fact that I'd done this weird thing and that the guy had even seemed to get what I was doing was a tipoff that I was on to something. So I took this picture of the bird in a tree and put it in a tree, and it turned out to be a small, nice moment in my movie that wouldn't have happened otherwise.

I try to keep all of my art and all of my life flexible enough that I can allow in these moments of accidental luck and inspiration. I wanted a picture of flowers but they had a picture of a bird, so of course a bird is what was right. We look for information to come to us in precise and logical ways, but you have to be open to moments like this. You have to practice being methodically open the way you would practice anything else, like math.

Picking up pieces of paper off the ground is a way of staying in practice. Most of the time it's just a receipt or something boring, but that doesn't matter, you're not dumb for turning it over. If you stick to the practice of picking up each little scrap, good things will come. It's also connected to writing. When I'm writing and my writing's not going very well, I begin to feel desperate. I'll take a walk around the block, and something I see—or a conversation I overhear—or something I find on the ground—always provides a spark. It's like we're all aliens, and we need to collect these found moments and artifacts as little reminders of what it's like to be human.

CENTRAL REESE SERVICE STATION

K.C. Johnson

K.C. Johnson is a beat reporter for the *Chicago Tribune*. He covers the Chicago Bulls and the NBA.

The slip of paper is no bigger than a business card; the numbers have weathered the passage of time well despite being scrawled in pencil.

I discovered it in 1985 while checking each pants pocket for leftovers—as my mother had taught me—as I dutifully performed my chore of washing the family laundry. My father's blue chinos smelled of oil and sweat. The white paper had smudge marks above the numbers.

I tucked the slip into my own back pocket and thought about how my friends' fathers had their work pants laundered at dry cleaners.

My father toiled in the business world for thirty years. He worked his way up to operations manager for a hospital supply company despite his lack of a college education. When the layoffs came, a palpable sense of doom entered our household. The weathered gold recliner in the corner of our living room held a broken man, his Stroh's beer cans resting on cork coasters nearby.

When another position in the same field ended for him after eighteen months because the company folded, the last of my father's self-confidence disappeared as well. His wife served as the primary breadwinner. His three children continued to overachieve.

My father insisted he loved us even as he said he had failed us. That's when he took the job at the gas station.

A **FRIEND, MORE OUT OF** niceness than need, offered him a steady job that was short on salary and long on monotony. When car tires ran over the hose near the driveway, the bell would ring inside the attendants' waiting room and my father would go fill 'er up, maybe check the oil or monitor the tire pressure.

Each Friday, my father would come home with a wad of cash in his pocket and a brown bag full of beer. He'd drop his white shirt next to the blue pants in the dirty-laundry pile. He owned three of each, which meant that laundry had to be done twice a week. After I'd washed the shirts, the blue patches—one that read CENTRAL REESE SERVICE STATION, and another that read KEN—looked sharp against the clean white fabric.

High school can be a cruel place. I'd hear the taunts of "grease monkey" in the cafeteria. While dressing for basketball practice I'd feel the eyes on me when somebody would announce that my father had gassed up his car. I'd avoid the conversations about fathers' careers or graduation presents.

I didn't grasp the lessons of hard work or commitment to family or strength in swallowing pride that our situation now presented. I only knew that my father no longer attended my after-school baseball games and that our conversations were short and strained because of my embarrassment.

One day my father forgot his lunch, and I took it to him on my way to school. I stopped short of the station and watched him interact with a customer, her smile still evident through her windshield as she drove away. Then came another car, and I heard a laugh as the driver rolled down his window and shook my father's hand.

Five years later, shortly after I graduated college, my parents moved away from our hometown. A few weeks after my father's last day of work, the owner mailed him a framed drawing of the station, with the pumps out front, the cars on risers in the mechanic's shed.

Close to 250 customers had signed the present. Three notes still resonate, perfectly capturing my father's grumpy act and soft heart:

> *You leave and the real estate values already have changed. You've been gone a short time and we ain't missed you yet.—Don Scott*

> *There's no one here to insult me. Miss you already.—Dody*

> *Our tires need checking. Ruth and I want you to take the first plane out. The window is now an empty spot where you used to stand. We always will miss seeing you there. Who will watch Central Street?—George Stevenson*

I never showed my father the slip of paper I found in his pocket or asked what the numbers meant. Perhaps they were a measure of tire pressure or gallons of gas or the amount of money brought in during his shift.

Their literal meaning doesn't really matter, but their significance to me is this: Occasionally, I lift the slip of paper from my desk drawer not merely to look at, but to touch and to feel the distance between ignorance and wisdom, shame and pride, hate and love.

Justin Gatlieb

Betsy Ross sewed the first american flag.

George washington was the first american president.

George washington was a general in the war.

martin luther king was a civil rights leader

chris columbus discovered America.

George washington ~~is he is is~~ cut down his fathers cherry tree with an axe his father gave to him for his birthday.

The ~~cout the~~ Black Panther was started During ~~a~~ the Vietnam war.

the sputnik sattelite was launched

man went ~~to~~ to outer space

Malcolm X began His quest for freedom

The ~~cost~~ constitution was sighned

The Boston tea Party Happened

the anti~~sed~~ government group, the anarchy was started

King Tuts tomb was discovered

the stop light was invented

the 1967 Ford Mustang shelby was introduced

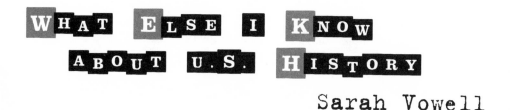

WHAT ELSE I KNOW ABOUT U.S. HISTORY

Sarah Vowell

Sarah Vowell is a journalist, humorist, and frequent contributor to the radio program *This American Life*. Her books include *Assassination Vacation* and *The Wordy Shipmates*.

Justin Gotlieb clearly knows his stuff. I mean: *Nitrous oxide was allowed to be used in muscle cars, show cars, and modified racing cars, for use in drag racing in 1978*? Now, that was a fine, fine moment in U.S. history. And yet, for all of Justin's comprehensiveness, he's let slip a few glaring omissions. I'm happy to pick up his slack.

□ **Tom Petty is on *Saturday Night Live*, and when the camera pans back to his drummer it turns out to be Dave Grohl.** Yes, for some unexplained reason, Dave Grohl was playing drums for Tom Petty. I remember thinking, *Hey, look, it's Dave Grohl!* But nothing about it was ever mentioned.

□ **Herman Melville writes, in one of his lengthy letters to his friend Nathaniel Hawthorne, that he wishes he had a paper mill in his house that continually made new paper so he'd never have to stop writing the letter.** I just love imagining Hawthorne receiving this entirely insane letter from his somewhat unhinged friend. I mean, Melville had already been sending him these letters that *seemed* endless, and now he was dreaming of writing him one that was *actually* endless.

- ◘ ***Dances with Wolves* beats out *Goodfellas* for the Best Picture Oscar.** This is one of the great tragedies of American history—not just a tragedy but an unfair blow to the ideals of democracy. I don't know if we as a nation will ever get over this.

- ◘ **J. Robert Oppenheimer watches the first atomic bomb test in the desert, and says, "Now I am become death, the destroyer of worlds."** Okay, if I'd just created the thing that could blow up the world, I don't know that a citation from the Bhagavad Gita would be the first words from my mouth.

- ◘ ***Buffy the Vampire Slayer* is canceled.** Oppenheimer had nothing on the careless, reckless execs who destroyed the world of *Buffy the Vampire Slayer*.

- ◘ **Truman Capote's *In Cold Blood* is published.** This book kind of ruined for everyone the allure of living out in the country. It's Capote's fault that every time I stay at a house in the country, I lie awake all night wondering if anyone will hear my screams.

- ◘ ***The Addams Family* theme song gives birth to the word "ooky."** No one will ever again be left floundering for a word to rhyme with "spooky."

- ◘ **As Al Gore concedes the 2000 election on national TV, his concession speech knocks *The West Wing* off the air.** That night, we lost both our good fictional President and our good real President, the most crushing double whammy of my lifetime. Justin Gotlieb, may you never know this kind of pain.

nitrous oxide was allowed to be
used in muscle cars ~~and~~ show cars, and
modified racing cars, for use in Drag racing
in ~~~~ 1978.

Black People won the right for
freedom

Hitler began the Nazi clan.

Ted Bondy was sentenced, then ~~~~
commited suicide.

Richard chase was murdered

JFK was assasanoted

Richie valins died in a plane crash

Edgar Allem Poe's short stories and
Poems were published

Elvis Died of a D.O.D.

Jimi Hendrix died

Jim morrison died.

Paul mcartney was Knighted

Justin Gotlieb was Born

D.T.

Drawing based on photo booth picture found by
Amy Shearn, Brooklyn, NY

PHOTO ME

Amy Shearn

Amy Shearn is the author of the novel *How Far Is the Ocean from Here*.
She lives in Brooklyn, New York.

We endure the machine's tidy explosions of light, grinning for pictures that I hope will not expose the mood I am trying hard to keep secret, and then we tumble back out into the muddled dark of the bar and right away Alex fingers the slot for our photos. "They're not there yet," I say, as he comes away with something between his thumb and index.

"Treasure!" he says. He looks at the photo for a second, not letting me see, and then pronounces, "Ha." It's like he's reading the word "ha" off of some invisible cue card, and it sounds nothing like actually laughing. He shows me a picture of two strangers from the photo booth and whispers, "Look, it's you! It's us!" and my brain turns a corner without me.

"What?" I say, as someone shushes me. It's *that* kind of show. The musician who's playing guitar and singing is a guy whose music I used to love but who I've just now realized is actually really boring. People are sitting down, for chrissakes, on the floor in front of the stage, listening quietly. *What a bunch of adults we all are*, I think, depressed.

"It's bizarre-o us," Alex says.

There are many things I like about Alex, but right now I can't seem to think of any of them. I have thoughts sometimes that are so mean that I worry about whether someone nearby is a mind reader and will read my mind and know how nasty I am. "What?" I say again, humanely, in a low, adult-alternative-folk-rock-friendly tone.

"They're just a slightly different version of us. Oh, that's hilarious," Alex says, laughlessly.

I study the photo. "This doesn't look anything like us."

"Are you kidding? It totally does. Look at that girl." He smashes his fingertip to her face, then looks around the bar as if trying to find her. "She looks just like you."

"Like *me*?" I look at the girl and look at Alex and look at the girl again. My eyes heat up and I accidentally picture them imploding like overcooked cherry tomatoes. "Are *you* kidding? What, you mean because she has brown hair and glasses? Is this what I look like? Look at her nose!"

This keeps happening to me lately—people keep telling me that I look like other people who strike me as being strange-looking or even homely—and now coming from Alex, with whom I'd thought I might really be on to something, well, I admit that I find it upsetting. Is this Alex's way of trying to let me know that I'm not as attractive as he thinks I may have been led to believe? Is he worried that I've developed some kind of false confidence, that too much flattery has brewed in me an unrealistic worldview? And: If no one can even see the difference between this girl and me, then why do I worry about the way I look so much—why does anyone worry? Who really looks at us?

It is true that we have the same dark-framed glasses, the girl and I, but lots of girls do. We were all told, during the time she was initially famous, that we looked like Lisa Loeb. We were all annoyed, even though we knew it was meant to be a compliment. We've all been asked by strangers, "But what if you took off your glasses, just for a second . . . ?" And it is also true that we have similar hair. It's not like it's spectacular hair of any kind. It's brown, of indeterminate length. It's just hair. But look at her button nose, at her lashless little eyes!

"Whatever," Alex says agreeably. He strangles his beer bottle by the neck, as if it had wronged him. Then he sticks his finger in the photo slot again. The machine is unresponsive. I start to understand why the previous couple gave up on waiting, or how you could forget about your photos if you had something better going on. The song ends and everyone claps and another song starts and everyone claps some more. "But this guy definitely looks exactly like me. God, it's really kind of fucked up. Dude looks *just* like me!"

It is a photo booth with modern options, the kind meant more for a train station, I think, than for recreation. We'd had a classic fun-house black-and-white strip in mind and had almost not even done the photo booth because of it, and now I see that we were right to think we shouldn't have. The time stamp at the bottom of the square photo is dated from nearly an hour ago and, because it has just turned midnight, yesterday. Because of this change in date our photo will be stamped with a famous and ominous date, 9/11, but their photo seems like just any other day. Everything is better on their side of midnight.

I take the photo and examine it more closely. Her arm is slung comfortably around his shoulders, her head tilted in toward his and looming slightly larger. She has a nicer smile than me and an open, kinder face. Maybe she is prettier than me after all. She looks—this oversized, rounder, happier version of me—as if she might cheerily devour her mate whole. They look unnaturally healthy and strangely platonic—the buddy-buddy arm-over-shoulder pose, the "friends forever" forehead tilt—and something about the way they both bare their teeth at the camera, looking somehow more like two people side by side than like a couple, makes me wonder if they aren't just friends mugging for the robotic camera.

"I don't think he looks anything like you," I say, careful to filter the crabbiness out of my voice. And really this is the main point here. Maybe I can admit that the girl looks a little like me. Maybe that's okay. I think I'm prettier than she is—my nose is more refined, my eyes more almond shaped, but, okay, whatever, maybe I'm just being vain—but this man certainly does not favor Alex. This man, objectively, despite whatever fondness I feel for my companion of these last few months and who knows how much longer, all tastes and preferences aside, is much more attractive than Alex. It's unquestionable. Alex has his charms. He has personality. He knows how to work what he's got. But what he's got is not what this guy's got. This man is blandly but undeniably attractive. He could be on television. He could play a nice guy in a movie. I can see, vaguely, the similarities that Alex is talking about. They are both white, and they both have brown hair. But this is assuredly not what Alex sees when he looks in the mirror.

Or is it? Is this why he is possessed of such rangy confidence, why he is always dating pretty girls, why he thinks it's okay to point out girls to me while we are somewhere together? And now I'm really starting to wonder (or maybe it's the tumult of beer and noise shipwrecking around in my brain): If Alex thinks this is what he looks like, and that that is what I look like, then he must think we are mismatched, and not in the way that I think we are mismatched, and that this is the secret he's been holding like a winning round of cards, fanned close in front of his heart, and this is the small but tangible ice spot I've been sensing between us, the doorstop keeping us decisively in the casual-dating waiting room, stuttering all relationship-oriented progress. There must be some way to tell him how wrong he is, that if this relationship is lopsided, pal, it's in the other direction. Right? Isn't it?

The singer finally launches into his famous-ish song and everyone goes very politely nuts. This is the slow, sad song that each of us feels expresses his or her own hidden, innermost thoughts on love more eloquently and accurately than any other song. I say to Alex, "Look—you don't look anything like John Ritter and this guy looks just exactly like John Ritter. Or, really, like a more handsome John Ritter."

Alex gropes around for our photo for the seventieth time and says, "John Ritter? The guy from *Three's Company*? He doesn't look anything like that guy," and I say, "Yes. Yes, Alex, he does," and he responds with the worst Don Knotts impersonation I have ever heard, sort of half Pee-wee Herman and half asphyxiating horse, and I feel embarrassed for him, for me, for all of us, Don Knotts included, because Don Knotts probably worked very hard to do Mr. Furley exactly how he did it, and how insulting, how devastating, to discover that a person like Alex completely misses all the nuances that made Don Knotts Don Knotts and not some second-rate impostor. It's like me and this girl—what the fuck? Has Alex ever noticed anything, ever really seen a single thing, in his entire blinded life? Can he really not tell how obviously hugely different from each other this girl and I are? I've never slung my arm like that around anyone's shoulders, not once! I would never have the confidence or pizzazz or whatever it is that allows one to streak my hair with those chunky yellow high-lights or wear bold bronze earrings—and yet each of these decisions that is or isn't made ends up meaning exactly nothing because no one notices anyway, and apparently me and this complete stranger, my exact opposite almost, are utterly interchangeable. The song ends and another song starts and my already undistinguished beer has gone tepid and flat but I have nowhere to put it down, and the stupid photo booth won't spit out my stupid photo—no *wonder* they abandoned theirs—and now I don't even want to go home with Alex anymore. I don't want to do anything with anyone at all.

But just then our photo is born into the little metal bed, glistening with chemical afterbirth. Alex takes it and flaps it around unnecessarily and we look at it and I hold up the old photo and say, "See? Nothing alike! See? They don't look anything like us at all!" And Alex just laughs at me and says, "Fine, you win."

Later, as we're getting ready to leave, I'm in line for the bathroom and I see the handsomer–John Ritter guy standing by the bar, holding two coats. "Here," I say, handing him the picture. I am trying to locate myself in the dark. The words unspool from somewhere in the back of my throat: "I think this is yours."

"Oh, thanks," he says. I shrug and then the bathroom door opens and out she comes.

THE QUEEN OF HAIGHT STREET

Kori Gardner

Kori Gardner is one half of the band Mates of State; the other half is her husband, Jason Hammel. Their latest album is called *Re-Arrange Us*.

One of our very first shows in San Francisco was at a club on Haight Street. Jason and I had just moved to California, and even though we knew the venue kind of sucked, we were still excited.

When it was time for us to play, Jason was nowhere to be found—I looked for him in the basement, in the boys' room, but it was like he'd been beamed into space. Finally he appeared, and we played our show for three people: the bartender and the two friends we'd invited. It was a deflating end to weeks of excitement about the gig.

After the show I asked Jason where he'd been beforehand, as though his disappearing act was responsible for the disappearance of our audience as well. Jason told me he'd been out on Haight Street, chatting it up with a crowd of friendly bums and bag ladies. A while later I went outside to get some air and an old woman pushing a grocery cart filled with junk approached me. She had tears in her eyes. She explained that she'd been hanging out in front of that particular club for years, listening to various bands play. "Usually it's terrible and I go about my business," she said. "But tonight, the music was so beautiful that

I cried." She said she would've paid to get in if she'd had the money, and I told her I would've made sure she'd gotten in had I known she was standing outside listening.

"I want to give you something," she said. She dug through her cart for a few minutes, tossing things over her shoulder like a mad scientist. At last, she produced a tiny purple crystal the size of a dime. "I found this years ago," she said. "It's very important to me—it's my most prized possession—and I want you to have it and keep it with you wherever you play."

And I always do. It's the most valuable treasure I own.

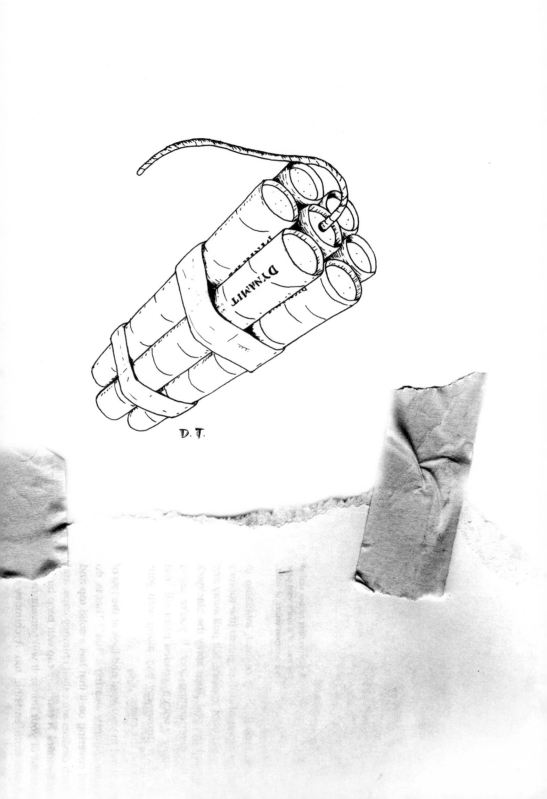

D. T.

THE NEXT BUILDING I PLAN TO BOMB

Charles Baxter

Charles Baxter is the author of five collections of stories and essays and five novels, including *First Light*, *The Feast of Love*, and most recently *The Soul Thief*. He is also a professor of creative writing at the University of Minnesota.

In the parking lot next to the bank, Harry Edmonds saw a piece of gray scrap paper the size of a greeting card. It had blown up next to his leg and attached itself to him there. Across the top margin was some scrabby writing in purple ink. He picked it up and examined it. On the upper left-hand corner someone had scrawled the phrase: THE NEXT BUILDING I PLAN TO BOMB. Harry unfolded the paper and saw an inked drawing of what appeared to be a sizable train station or some other public structure, perhaps an airport terminal. In the drawing were arched windows and front pillars but very little other supporting detail. The building looked solid, monumental, and difficult to destroy.

He glanced around the parking lot. There he was in Five Oaks, Michigan, where there were no such buildings. In the light wind other pieces of paper floated by in an agitated manner. One yellow flyer was stuck to a fire hydrant. On the street was the usual crowd of bankers, lawyers, shoppers, and students. As usual, no one was watching him or paying much attention to him. He put the piece of paper into his coat pocket. All afternoon, while he sat at his desk, his hand traveled down to his pocket to touch the drawing. Late in the day, half as a joke, he showed the paper to the office receptionist. "You've got to take it to the police," she told him. "This is dangerous. This is the work of a maniac. That's LaGuardia there, the airport? In the picture? I was there last month. I'm sure it's LaGuardia, Mr. Edmonds. No kidding. Definitely LaGuardia."

So at the end of the day, before going home, he drove to the main police station on the first floor of City Hall. Driving into the sun, he felt his eyes squinting against the burrowing glare. He had stepped inside the front door when the waxy bureaucratic smell of the building hit him and gave him an immediate headache. A cop in uniform, wearing an impatient expression, sat behind a desk, shuffling through some papers, and at that moment it occurred to Harry Edmonds that if he showed what was in his pocket to the police he himself would become a prime suspect and an object of intense scrutiny, all privacy gone. He turned on his heel and went home.

AT DINNER, HE SAID TO his girlfriend, "Look what I found in a parking lot today." He handed her the drawing.

Lucia examined the soiled paper, her thumb and finger at its corner, and said, "The next building I plan to bomb." Her tone was light and urbane. She sold computer software and was sensitive to gestures. Then she said, "That's Union Station, in Chicago." She smiled. "Well, Harry, what are you going to do with this? Some nutcase did this, right?"

"Actually, I got as far as the foyer in the police station this afternoon," he said. "Then I turned around. I couldn't show it to them. I thought they'd suspect me or something."

"Oh, that's so melodramatic," she said. "You've never committed a crime in your life. You're a banker, for Chrissake. You're in the trust department. You're harmless."

Harry sat back in his chair and looked at her. "I'm not that harmless."

"Yes, you are," she laughed. "You're quite harmless."

"Lucia," he said. "I wish you wouldn't use that word."

"Harmless? It's a compliment."

"Not in this country, it isn't," he said.

On the table were the blue plates and matching napkins and the yellow candles that Lucia brought out whenever she was proud of what she or Harry had cooked. Today it was Burmese chicken curry. "Well, if you're worried, take it to the cops," Lucia told him. "That's what the cops are there for. Honey," she said, "no one will suspect you of anything. You're handsome and stable and you're my sweetie, and I love you, and what else happened today? Put that awful, creepy paper back into your pocket. How do you like the curry?"

"It's delicious," he said.

AFTER HARRY HAD GOTTEN UP his nerve sufficiently to enter the police station again, he walked in a determined manner toward the front desk. After looking carefully at the drawing and the inked phrase, and writing down Harry Edmonds's name and address, the officer, whose badge identified him as Sergeant Bursk, asked, "Mr. Edmonds, you got any kids?"

"Kids? No, I don't have any kids. Why?"

"Kids did this," Sergeant Bursk told him, waving the paper in front of him as if he were drying it off. "My kids could've done this. Kids do this. Boys do this. They draw torture chambers and they make threats and what-have-you. That's what they do. It's the youth. But they're kids. They don't mean it."

"How do you know?"

"Because I have three of them," Sergeant Bursk said. "I'm not saying that you should have kids, I'm just saying that I have them. I'll keep this drawing, though, if you don't mind."

"Actually," Harry said, "I'd like it back."

"Okay," Sergeant Bursk said, handing it to him, "but if we hear of any major bombings, and, you know, large-scale serious death, maybe we'll give you a call."

"Yeah," Harry said. He had been expecting this. "By the way," he asked, "does this look like any place in particular to you?"

The cop examined the picture. "Sure," he said. "That's Grand Central. In New York, on Forty-second Street, I think. I was there once. You can tell by the clock. See this clock here?" He pointed at a vague circle. "That's Grand Central, and this is the big clock that they've got there on the front."

"**T**HE **FUCK** **IT** **IS.**" **THE** kid said. The kid was in bed with Harry Edmonds in the Motel 6. They had found each other in a bar downtown and then gone to this motel, and after they were finished, Harry drew the drawing out of his pants pocket on the floor and showed it to him. The kid's long brown hair fell over his eyes and, loosened from its ponytail, spread out on the pillow. "I know this fucking place," the kid said. "I've, like, traveled, you know, all over Europe. This is in Europe, this place, this is fucking Deutschland we're talking about here." The kid got up on his elbows to see better. "Oh yeah, I remember this place. I was there, two summers ago? Hamburg? This is the Dammtor Bahnhof."

"Never heard of it," Harry Edmonds said.

"You never heard of it 'cause you've never been there, man. You have to fucking be there to know about it." The kid squinched his eyebrows together like a professor making a difficult point. "A *bahnhof*, see, is a train station, and the Dammtor Bahnhof is, like, one of the stations there, and this is the one the Nazis rounded up the Jews to. And, like, sent them off from. This place, man. Absolutely. It's still standing. This one, it fucking deserves to be bombed. Just blow it totally the fuck away, off the face of the earth. That's just my opinion. It's evil, man."

The kid moved his body around in bed, getting himself comfortable again after stating his opinions. He was slinky and warm, like a cat. The kid even made back-of-the-throat noises, a sort of satisfied purr.

"**I** **THOUGHT** **WE** **WERE** **FINISHED** with that," Harry's therapist said, "I thought we were finished with the casual sex. I thought, Harry, that we had worked through those fugitive impulses. I must tell you that it troubles me that we haven't. I won't say that we're back to square one, but it is a backwards step. And what I'm wondering now is, why did it happen?"

"Lucia said I was harmless, that's why."

"And did that anger you?"

"You bet it angered me." Harry sat back in his chair and looked directly at his therapist. He wished she would get a new pair of eyeglasses. These eyeglasses made her look like one of those movie victims killed within the first ten minutes, right after the opening credits. One of those innocent bystanders. "Bankers are not harmless," he said. "I can assure you."

"Then why did you pick up that boy?" She waited. When he didn't say anything, she said, "I can't think of anything more dangerous to do."

"It was the building," Harry said.

"What building?"

"I showed Lucia the building. On the paper. This paper." He took it out of his pocket and handed it to his therapist. By now the paper was becoming soft and wrinkled. While she studied the picture, Harry watched the second hand of the wall clock turn.

"You found this?" she asked. "You didn't draw this."

"Yes, I found it." He waited. "I found it in the parking lot six blocks from here."

"All right. You showed Lucia this picture. And perhaps she called you harmless. Why did you think it so disturbing to be called harmless?"

"Because," Harry said, "in this country, if you're harmless, you get killed and eaten. That's the way things are going these days. That's the current trend. I thought you had noticed. Perhaps not."

"And why do you say that people get killed and eaten? That's an extravagant metaphor. It's a kind of hysterical irony."

"No, it isn't. I work in a bank and I see it happen every day. I mop up the blood."

"I don't see what this has to do with picking up young men and taking them to motels," she said. "That's back in the country of acting out. And what I'm wondering is, what does this mean about your relationship to Lucia? You're endangering her, you know." As if to emphasize the point, she said, "It's wrong, what you did. And very, very dangerous. With all your thinking, did you think about that?"

Harry didn't answer. Then he said, "It's funny. Everybody has a theory about what the building is. You haven't said anything about it. What's your theory?"

"This building?" Harry's therapist examined the paper through her movie-victim glasses. "Oh, it's the Field Museum, in Chicago. And that's not a theory. It *is* the Field Museum."

O**N TUESDAY NIGHT, AT 3 A.M.** Harry fixed his gaze on the bedroom ceiling. There, as if on a screen, shaped by the light through the curtains luffing in the window, was a public building with front pillars and curved arched windows and perhaps a clock. On the ceiling the projected sun of Harry's mind rose wonderfully, brilliantly gold, one or two mind-wisp cumulus clouds passing from right to left across it, but not so obscured that its light could not penetrate the great public building into which men, women, and children—children in strollers, children hand in hand with their parents—now filed, shadows on the ceiling, lighted shadows, and for a moment Harry saw an explosive flash.

Harry Edmonds lay in his bed without sleeping. Next to him was his girlfriend, whom he had planned to marry, once he ironed out a few items of business in his personal life and settled them. He had made love to her, this woman, this Lucia, a few hours earlier, with earnest caresses, but now he seemed to be awake again. He rose from bed and went down to the kitchen. In the harsh fluorescence he ate a cookie and on an impulse turned on the radio. The radio blistered with the economy of call-in hatred and religion revealed to rabid-mouthed men who now gasped and screamed into all available microphones. He adjusted the dial to a call-in station. Speaking from Delaware, a man said, "There's a few places I'd do some trouble to, believe me, starting with the Supreme Court and moving on to a clinic or two." Harry snapped off the radio.

N**OW HE SITS IN THE** light of the kitchen. He feels as dazed as it is possible for a sane man to feel at three-thirty in the morning. *I am not silly, nor am I trivial,* Harry says to himself, as he reaches for a pad of paper and a no. 2 pencil. At the top of the pad, Harry writes, "The next place I plan to bomb," and then very slowly, and with great care, begins to draw his own face, its smooth, cleanshaven contours, its courteous half-smile. When he perceives his eyes beginning to water, he rips off the top sheet with his picture on it and throws it in the wastebasket. The refrigerator seems to be humming some tune to him, some tune without a melody, and he flicks off the overhead light before he recognizes that tune.

IT IS MIDDAY IN DOWNTOWN Five Oaks, Michigan, the time for lunch and rest and conversation, and for a remnant, a lucky few, it may be a time for love, but here before us is Harry Edmonds, an officer in the trust department at Southeastern Michigan Bank and Trust, standing on a street corner in a strong spring wind. The wind pulls at his tie and musses his hair. Nearby, a recycling container appears to have overturned, and sheets of paper, hundreds of them, papers covered with drawings and illustrations and words, have scattered. Like a flock of birds, they have achieved flight. All around Harry Edmonds they are gripped in this whirlwind and flap and snap in circles. Some stick to him. There are glossy papers with perfumed inserts, and there are yellowing papers with four-color superheroes, and there are the papers with attractive unclothed air-brushed bodies, and there are the papers with bills and announcements and loans. Here are the personals, swirling past, and there a flyer for a home theater big-screen TV. Harry Edmonds, a man uncertain of the value of his own life, who at this moment does not know whether his life has, in fact, any importance at all, or any future, lifts his head in the wind, increasing in volume and intensity, and for a moment he imagines himself being blown away.

From across the street, the way he raises his head might appear, to an observer, as a posture of prayer. God, it is said, resides in the whirlwind, and certainly Harry Edmonds's eyes are closed and now his head is bowed. He does not move forward or backward, and it is unclear from the expression on his face whether he is making any sort of wish. He remains stationary, on this street corner, while all about him the papers fly first toward him, and then away.

A moment later he is gone from the spot where he stood. No doubt he has returned to his job at the bank, and that is where we must leave him.

FINDING the Diary of TAMMY PIERCE

By Esther Pearl Watson

Esther Pearl Watson is an artist living in Los Angeles. Her comics are featured regularly in *Bust Magazine*, and her book, *Unlovable Vol. 1*, is available through Fantagraphics.

IN 1995, MY HUSBAND AND I WERE DRIVING FROM LAS VEGAS to SAN FRANCISCO.

WE TOOK THE SHORT CUT THROUGH DEATH VALLEY-- IN THE SUMMER!

WE HAD to DRIVE with the HEAT ON AND the WINDOWS DOWN. THIS WAS THE ONLY WAY MY CAR WOULD NOT OVERHEAT.

MY CAR STEREO HAD BEEN STOLEN 3 TIMES. I HAD GIVEN UP REPLACING IT. SO WE LISTENED to MIXED TAPES ON THE BOOMBOX.

THEN THE BATTERIES RAN OUT.

AFTER A WHILE, WE WERE HOT, THIRSTY AND BORED.

REALLY, REALLY BORED.

WE FINALLY SAW A GAS STATION AND PLANNED TO BUY MORE BATTERIES.

DURING A QUICK RUN TO THE WOMEN'S RESTROOM...

I noticed SOMEONE had LEFT A DIARY ON THE SINK.

The diary was eight years old and had secret code.

I KEPT A DIARY DURING the same YEARS.

THERE WAS NO way I could LEAVE it behind!

I tRiED to act NATURAL.

THE DIARY BEGAN WITH AN OBSESSIVE LONGING FOR A GUY WHO WAS OUT OF TOWN.

WE WERE SO SICK OF READING ABOUT THIS GUY WHO DIDN'T SEEM TO NOTICE HER.

AFTER WHAT SEEMED TO BE FIFTY MILES, SHE FORGOT ABOUT TIM STARRY.

SHE BEGAN TO FOCUS ON TWO GUYS. (WE HAD OUR FAVORITE.)

ONE WAS THIS CREEPY GUY WHO RUBBED HER BACK AND GAVE BAD PICK-UP LINES.

The Smiths

THE OTHER WAS THIS PERFECT GUY NEXT DOOR WHO CONSOLED HER WHEN SHE TALKED TO HIM ABOUT LIFE.

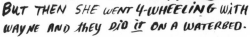

BUT THEN SHE WENT 4-WHEELING WITH WAYNE AND THEY DID IT ON A WATERBED.

SHE DIDN'T MENTION KEN AGAIN.

THE DIARY ENDED WHEN SHE WENT TO DISNEYLAND. ALL PAGES AFTER WERE TORN OUT.

LONDON BOROUGH OF BROMLEY

Beaverwood School for Girls. Headmistress: Mrs. E. Wilkinson, BA.
_____

Beaverwood Road, Perry Street, Chislehurst.   01-300 3156

23rd November, 1982.

To all Sixth Form Parents.

SPEECH DAY, 1982.

Following our Senior Speech Day, I should like to
apologise for any offence that Miss Fairbairns, our Guest Speaker,
may have given.

When we invite a guest to speak at any school function,
we try to find someone who is accustomed to young people and in
addition has something interesting to say. I am sure you would
agree that a novelist who has also been a 'Writer in Residence'
in Bromley Schools, would seem to be a good choice.

I am sure it is unnecessary for me to say that in no
way did Miss Fairbairns' remarks reflect the philosophy of the
school.

Yours sincerely,

E. Wilkinson

Headmistress.

SPEECH DAY, 1982

David Shrigley

David Shrigley, an artist based in Glasgow, is the author of many books, including *Blank Page and Other Pages* and *Drawings Done on the Phone Whilst Talking to an Idiot.*

I have a friend who works in a Salvation Army charity shop in London. He finds all kinds of things in the pockets of donated coats and sends them on to me. He's proved to be a real source of treasure.

The attraction of these found items is that they arrive context-free, separated from the situation in which they once, perhaps, made sense. My imagination is obliged to fill the gaps. Maybe in a small way this is an example of what makes good storytelling—giving the audience just enough so that they can finish the story themselves.

We will never know what subversive, amoral thesis was at the core of poor Miss Fairbairns's speech, and if we actually discovered the context into which these fragments fit, they wouldn't necessarily become less intriguing. Perhaps it's not only the absence of context but also the fact that these events have been documented in such an official way that make it all seem so absurd. Or maybe the event was even more absurd in reality.

It's the inconsistency of our attempts at communication, that space between what we intend to say and how we are understood, that makes language such a delight.

THE BLOODY JOCKSTRAP INCIDENT

Jenji Kohan

Jenji Kohan is the creator of the television show *Weeds*.

Like a lot of my friends, I absolutely love shopping at thrift stores. I'm mesmerized by old family photo albums, letters I find tucked into books, and even the old games and toys I come across that people would've killed for at the time they came out, now dusty and lonely next to a broken blender on a low shelf. It's always a big treasure hunt for me. My husband, Christopher, has always been less excited about it. He has trouble separating the items found at thrift stores from the stories of how they got there. I'm always intrigued by the human experiences hovering behind an old chipped World's Greatest Grandpa mug or a taped-up box of Mastermind. *Who did this stuff belong to?* I see it as a thrilling, imaginative form of urban archaeology. For Chris, the stories conjured up are mostly tragic and revolve around people in desperate situations—getting evicted and having to leave all their stuff behind—and death. Still, when we were young and freshly dating, he'd always indulge me and come along anytime I went out on one of my daylong thrift-store treasure hunts.

This all came to an end in Las Vegas. Chris and I had rented a Chevy Suburban with some friends and taken a road trip to Vegas to go thrifting. No gambling, just a full day of binge shopping at thrift stores; the ones in Vegas were always much less picked over than the thrift stores in L.A.

Late in the day, at one of those huge supersize stores, there was a bin where everything inside was a dollar. Chris was sifting through it when he pulled out a jockstrap, the kind of cotton ball-supporter an athlete would wear, but stained with dried blood around the ball region. It was both shocking and mystifying—I mean, how had this thing gotten here? What horrible form of torture had been inflicted on this mystery man's balls? And who had decided to price the jockstrap at a dollar?

Chris threw his hands up and said, "That's it! I'm done with this!" He marched out of the store, and I could never coax him into going thrifting with me again. We began to refer to this as The Bloody Jockstrap Incident. Every time I tried to get him to join me on one of my treasure hunts, he said he was still haunted by the image of some poor man's parts bleeding, wondering what kind of horrific sports injury had gone down. The idea of looking through people's former possessions made him unhappy and miserable. I was bummed because he'd always been my partner in crime, but I continued my thrifting ways for a while. Even when I was unemployed for long stretches, I could go on an all-day shopping spree, come home with bags of awesome stuff, and only have spent twenty-five dollars. It felt uniquely satisfying to find things that were so one-of-a-kind. Later, though, we started having kids, and I couldn't just spend the day roaming the city, looking for treasures. I started getting more work, which was a blessing, but it also cut into my hard-core thrifting.

Flash forward to 2005. Chris and I had just had our third kid, whom we adored, but who'd also been a surprise. Chris decided he wanted to get a vasectomy. "We'll just take the matter off the table," he reasoned. "We have enough children." I wasn't too thrilled about it, but Chris went in to have the operation, and the doctor explained to him that when they cut into his balls, they'd have to put a titanium clip on his vas deferens and that he'd need to wear a jockstrap for a few days to provide support for his balls.

That night, Chris sat in a big armchair in our living room, experiencing pain I could only imagine, dazed from a heavy dose of Vicodin, his balls resting on a bag of frozen peas wrapped in a dish towel. He was not a happy camper, and neither was I—I was mourning the loss of our family's fertility. We were both moody and lost in the gloom, when Chris suddenly reached down to adjust his jockstrap, saw these little bloodstains, and cried out, "Oh my God—Vegas! I know what happened!"

I looked at him and then I got it, too, and knew exactly what he meant. The bloody jockstrap in Las Vegas hadn't been the product of some bizarre, cruel torture—some other guy had simply gotten a vasectomy and his stained jockstrap had somehow ended up in the dollar bin at Value World. All the dots were instantly connected, and we stared at each other dumbfounded, and then began to laugh out loud, giddy from the epiphany, pulled free from our misery.

There was, of course, still the question of what to do with Chris's bloody jockstrap. It was important to both of us that it be disposed of properly so that it wouldn't end up in a thrift store somewhere and ruin another couple's thrift-store-shopping ritual. When Chris had healed up, we invited a few friends over and held a ceremonial throwing-away-of-the-bloody-jockstrap. Chris made a little toast. "This is going in the trash," he said. "No one else will ever have to imagine the things that I did."

And we all clinked our glasses.

BEST REGARDS, ROBERT ZIMMERMAN

David Simon

David Simon is the author of the book *Homicide: A Year on the Killing Streets* and creator of the television show *The Wire*.

Baltimore, 1988. I'd been a crime reporter for *The Sun* for about five years and decided it was time to write a book about the homicide investigation unit. The police department agreed to let me hang around during the midnight shift. Those hours could be painfully slow, but while the detectives would sit there, bored out of their minds, watching late-night TV or sleeping, I would spend hour after hour in the back, poring over old case files. In those days, the files were just long rows of three-by-five cards; on every card was either the name of the person killed or the person charged with the killing. The card would also list the case-file number, the date of the incident, the precinct where the killing went down, and where the file was stored. My hope was always to find enough information on the card to be able to hunt down the paperwork and learn more about a particular case.

Of course I paid special attention to the cases of the detectives whose stories I was following. When they told me about a good case, I'd immediately go look it up in the files. If I got the name of a celebrated gangster—someone like Squeaky Jordan, who I knew had done a lot of damage—I would practically run to the card file to pull up the cases he'd been involved with. For a reporter, this was an incredible treat: looking through homicide files and investigative files, reading things that weren't public information. I was like a kid in a candy store.

Over the course of a few months, I went through thousands and thousands of cards, from *A* to *Z*. I was taking voluminous notes because I knew at some point they were going to throw me out of the unit. I'd often work till dawn, frantically trying to record as much as I could in the short time I had. It was on one of these late nights that I finally got down to the *Z*s, and found a card with the infamous name: Zantzinger, William.

I**N 1963, BOB DYLAN RELEASED** his seminal album, *The Times They Are A-Changin'*. If you have this album, put it on and listen to track nine—"The Lonesome Death of Hattie Carroll." The opening lyrics: "William Zanzinger [*sic*] killed poor Hattie Carroll with a cane that he twirled around his diamond ring finger at a Baltimore hotel society gathering. . . ." It's not Dylan's most famous song, but I knew it well enough to understand what I'd discovered. By pure chance, I'd stumbled across the case-file card for the legendary death of Hattie Carroll.

Hattie Carroll was a fifty-one-year-old African American waitress who worked at the posh downtown Emerson Hotel. She was also a mother of eleven children and the president of a black social club. On February 9, 1963, Hattie Carroll had the misfortune of serving William Zantzinger, the twenty-four-year-old son of a wealthy, white tobacco farmer. When Zantzinger arrived at the restaurant he was already stumbling drunk. He proceeded to violently harass Hattie Carroll, striking her with a cane and calling her a "black bitch." Soon after Zantzinger struck her, Carroll told her coworkers, "I feel deathly ill, that man has upset me so," and then dropped dead of a heart attack. Zantzinger was originally charged with murder but ended up serving only six months on a manslaughter charge. Dylan forever memorialized the incident in his famous song.

A**S A LIFELONG DYLAN FAN,** I was dying to unearth the Zantzinger files, which seemed to represent an untold piece of rock-and-roll history. But at first, nobody could find them; they weren't in any of the regular drawers. Then I learned that they were being stored in the basement of the Central District Station, which was downtown, close to the old Emerson Hotel. Two weeks later, I had the files in my hands.

To my disappointment, it was all on microfilm. I'd fantasized about old, yellowed, crinkly copy paper, the kind of carbon paper they used in the department in the sixties. But still, the microfilm files contained everything I could've hoped for—one amazing witness statement after another. I discovered, for instance, that as the arresting officers were leading Zantzinger down the steps of the hotel, his wife, who was also blind-drunk, jumped on the back of one of the cops and knocked him down, screaming, "Don't take my Billy! He beats me but I love him so!" That cop injured his back in the takedown and never returned to active duty. It was unbelievable, all these Baltimore high-society names—the sons and daughters of that blue-blooded hierarchy—smeared across the pages. Most of them were genuinely shocked by Zantzinger's behavior. But some were a little skeptical of his culpability, perhaps with reason.

You see, Dylan didn't paint the most accurate portrait of what went down the night of February 9, 1963. Unquestionably, Zantzinger's behavior toward Hattie Carroll was unforgivable. But he did not beat her to death with a cane, as the song suggests. The cane he had was one of those little carnival canes, made of bamboo. He may have tapped her with it, but probably couldn't have done any real damage; there were no marks on her body. What killed Hattie, most likely, was the terrible humiliation and stress caused by Zantzinger's harsh words and obnoxious behavior. Hattie Carroll suffered from extreme hypertension; her autopsy report indicated she had an enlarged heart and high blood pressure and listed a brain hemorrhage as the official cause of death. So perhaps the lessening of his sentence from murder to manslaughter was not as criminal as Dylan's lyrics would have us believe. Nevertheless, the death of Hattie Carroll was a huge focus of the civil rights movement, and Zantzinger became the poster boy for racial cruelty; he was sentenced to six months' imprisonment on August 28, 1963, the same day Martin Luther King, Jr., led the March on Washington and delivered his famous "I Have a Dream" speech.

EVENTUALLY I GOT MY HANDS on the original case files for the Zantzinger case and spent night after night reading through them. It was the last page in the file that sent me into motion on a new wild search. It was a typed note to the chief inspector of Baltimore City Detectives, signed by the head of the Maryland State Police. It read: "Attached is a memo from a folk singer in New York named Mr. Zimmerman who is writing for information about the case. I believe this is handled by your agency, so I forwarded it to you. Best regards." Mr. Zimmerman. Robert Zimmerman. Bob Dylan.

My heart quickened. I could see that a piece of paper had at one time been stapled to the policeman's note, and then torn away—Dylan's original letter. I start leafing quickly back through the entire file, figuring that it had to be in there somewhere. Larceny was in my heart at that moment. A plan swirled to life in my head: I would xerox the letter and pocket the original. I would own this piece of rock-and-roll memorabilia. I went faster and faster through the pages, and finally reached the last sheet, and—*Christ!*—the letter was gone.

The missing Dylan letter became my Holy Grail. All I wanted was to find that letter from Robert Zimmerman to the Maryland State Police. It tormented me. I figured there were two people who knew about the letter—me and whoever had taken it. I felt clever for having discovered it, but whoever had the letter had been equally clever and first to the dance.

One night, I was hanging out with an old detective, a black guy from New York named Harry Edgerton. Edgerton was a music lover—his mother had played jazz piano. I cautiously brought up the Hattie Carroll case, and he said, "Oh, Zantzinger!" And he started to sing the song. Then he stopped and said, "Yeah, you didn't find the Dylan letter, did you?"

I was stunned. "How'd you know about that?"

"'Cause I was gonna lift it!" he cried. He started laughing. "As soon as I got to homicide, I pulled that file, just to read it. I saw that other letter, and I was like, 'Where is it? Where is it?' A letter signed by Robert Zimmerman? Tucked away here in one of these old drawers? Too late. Some fucking cop beat me to it."

After that, we spent a lot of nights speculating about who might have nabbed it. We'd be like, "You think it could've been Charlie Kearse?" "What about Billy Warden?" And then we'd crack up. But the mystery was impenetrable. The letter could've been taken anytime in the past couple of decades.

I started asking everyone if they had any clue what could've happened to it. "This didn't get xeroxed?" "No," they'd say, "we shipped all that stuff out to the Maryland State Archives years ago. We wouldn't have anything from 1963. We probably mimeographed it, put it on microfilm, and now it's gone."

But I couldn't accept that; I couldn't let the Dylan letter go. I spent another three or four months researching the case, trying to track it down. I wrote the Maryland Archives. I searched the court files, praying that maybe somehow it had gotten mixed in with the docket books. I researched twenty different ways from Sunday. But the letter never surfaced.

MONTHS **LATER, I WROTE A** story on Zantzinger around the twenty-fifth anniversary of Hattie Carroll's death. I had all the notes from my year in Homicide and all my subsequent research on the case. But I knew that to really do the story justice, I'd have to talk to the people involved, including Zantzinger. First, I reached Zantzinger's lawyer. He told me how libelous Dylan's song about Zantzinger was and said he'd fired a shot across Columbia Records' bow in 1964, threatening a lawsuit. After that, he said, Dylan stopped playing "The Lonesome Death of Hattie Carroll" at his shows for many years.

Eventually, Zantzinger agreed to meet with me. I found him living down in Charles County, working as a real estate broker. He would only let me talk to him off the record, but we spoke for a long, long time. As expected, he became belligerent when I brought up Carroll's death. "You people were here on the fifteenth anniversary, the twentieth, and now you come again on the twenty-fifth! What do you want from me?" I was ready to leave, to write him off as the man in the song, when he said something that moved me: "Listen, I know I'm responsible for that woman's death. I know that. You think I don't know that? I have to live with that every day of my life." It was in that moment that I understood that William Zantzinger would never rise to the level of villainy that I wanted from him, the William Zantzinger of Dylan's song. He was just a sad man, confined by history for what he had done in one youthful, stupid, drunken moment.

MY GUESS IS THAT SOME detective pocketed Dylan's letter before shipping off the files to the Maryland Archives. Robert Zimmerman may have been an unknown folksinger in 1963, but by 1968, when the case was sent to storage, everyone in America knew Bob Dylan. Some Baltimore cop has that letter, or his son does, or his grandson. I may never find my Holy Grail after all, but I do have my "find"—that original inquest from the head of the Maryland State Police to the chief inspector of Baltimore City Detectives. It's in a frame, on the wall above my desk. And I take some solace in the fact that twenty-five years after Dylan mailed his inquiry off to the police, I accomplished what he'd been attempting to do—I accessed those files myself. All those long nights, sifting through the case files, I solved my own small piece of the puzzle.

HOW I FOUND MY MOTHER

Bich Minh Nguyen

Bich Minh Nguyen is the author of a memoir, *Stealing Buddha's Dinner*, and a novel, *Short Girls*.

I must have been snooping through boxes in my parents' house, because there was no other way I would have found the photograph. This was 1995 or maybe 1994. It may have been summer, or winter break, me on a brief visit home from college. I know my father was renovating the house then because he's always renovating, drywall always half done, tiles stilled in their push across the kitchen floor.

In my parents' house nothing is ever really thrown away and every drawer turns into a junk drawer. There's a closet where we simply throw things— broken hangers, chewed-up dog toys—and slam the door shut. Better not to look. But I can picture my college self, alone in that never-done house, picking through the plastic bins my stepmother had stuffed with years of papers and receipts, and then, finding what I had never even searched for: a photograph of my mother.

On April 29, 1975, the night before Saigon fell, my family left Vietnam. We fled, my father and uncles and grandmother and sister and I, with literally the clothes on our backs. I was eight months old. At the time, my father and mother were separated, and she was living with her family in a different part of the city.

My father had no way to get in touch with her and no time to go after her. So we left. We were gone before she knew it. We took a chance because we had no other chance. We hoped for luck, and got it. Meaning: I grew up in the Midwest, in Michigan, in a family that never spoke of topics like sex or the war. I grew up with sitcoms that resolved problems just before the credits rolled, in a time of tapered pants and Aqua Net hair spray. I grew up with a stepmother and a grandmother. I grew up hardly thinking about my "real" mother at all.

THERE IS NO GOOD WAY to tell this story. It tends to elicit shock and pity. It is uncomfortably dramatic—and yet people always want it to be more dramatic. Because in truth, I never questioned my father. I didn't ask who or where my mother was, didn't go looking through his room. It was easier not to seek and not to find.

But then my mother found me. Eventually she made it to the United States on her own and sent my sister and me a letter. When I finally met my mother— in Boston, where she had landed a few years before—I was twenty years old. What did I expect? I didn't know. I knew nothing about my mother until the moment I saw her and she said, "Geez, you are *so* late." We went out for dim sum and walked around Chinatown and bought moon cakes. Nervous, I talked about the Boston Tea Party. She asked me about school, and we agreed that education, in general, was a very fine thing. We were on our best behavior, like two people on a blind date. "Let's stay in touch," we said.

And later that year, or the year after, I must have snooped through my parents' boxes, though I don't remember it, and that's when I found her, my mother, in a black-and-white photograph, taken when she was young, in Vietnam. She is posed outside a stone house near an open window. She is dressed up, in a satin flowered gown with three-quarter sleeves and a flaring skirt. Her hair is pulled back in a near-beehive updo. I don't know if I'd been born yet. Maybe my father took the picture and kept it all that time, crossing the world between Vietnam and Michigan, and all those years in which no one ever spoke of my mother.

WHAT DOES IT MEAN WHEN you forget how you found something? It means you want to have had it all along. It means you don't want to think about the loss that precedes the finding.

SUCH A STORY, MY MOTHER said once, over the phone, when I asked her how she and my father had first met.

Oh, she said. Why would you want to know *that*?

I asked her if she remembered the photograph, described it to her. No idea, she said. But do I look pretty?

AT HOME IN MICHIGAN MY father is on a constant quest to get as big of a television as he can afford. A forty-inch screen is, in his opinion, paltry. It's settling. We settle, down onto the old puffy leather sofas, to watch the action movies he loves. The half-painted living room fills with images of machine guns waving and spraying. Knives slashing. Fists hitting their mark. Cars smash onto sidewalks, fly in slow-motion arcs through the air.

It's late at night. It's 1994 or maybe 1995; it's last year, last summer, last month. My father and I watch TV; the volume is so loud there is no place in the house free of gunfire and grenades.

On the television screen: precision battle, blood. *Chet cha*, my father exclaims. *Holy wow.* Later he will fall asleep to these same scenes, unwilling to let the movie end or the television rest. Let's see it again, he'll say the next day, reaching for the remote control. I want to know how to pull back the days that have slipped from my grasp. I want to talk to my father, explain that I had to find that photograph in order to find *her*, to allow the portrait of her past into my present life. But he and I don't speak in such ways. I may never know if he knows I have this photo-graph, this document of the story we share. In his favorite movies, there is little dialogue, and the heroes have perfect balance. They fling themselves from build-ing to building as if they already know they're safe, that the resolution, the soft shore of the fade to black, is already waiting to welcome them into that beckon-ing landscape where all the avenues point forward.

ANIMAL HUSBANDRY

David Kirby

David Kirby is a National Book Award finalist who teaches poetry at
Florida State University. His books include *The Ha-Ha* and *The House of
Blue Light*.

I look up to see not only that someone has written

"I want to suck a cock" on the men's room wall

in the ribs joint just outside Thomasville but that

a helpful party has added "Suck your own—I do!"

whose cheerful advice draws the contempt of a third writer,

one who uses the correct South Georgia plural form

as he writes "HOMO'S" and, should anyone be in doubt

as to the objects of his ill will, draws an arrow toward

the pencilings of the two previous guests, leaving me

to think, not of sex of either the mutual or self-pleasuring

if decidedly acrobatic kind but of the plaques in front

of the houses announcing that this is the residence

of THE JONE'S, which surely has led at least one wag

of a solicitor to knock politely and ask, "May I

speak to the Jone?" thereby signaling his greater interest

in imparting a style lesson than in selling a rack

of high-end kitchen knives that are no better than

        the cheap kind or a set of encyclopedias that only

the most naive or guilt-tripped parent would buy

           since you can get everything on the Internet now,

    as well as all those restaurants that have named themselves

by adding an apostrophe and an s to a type of food,

      such as SANGRIA'S or PESTO'S, as though the place

    belonged, not to an over-the-hill athlete or a Japanese

cartel or a bunch of former frat brothers who decided

        it'd be more fun to own a business where they could eat

for free and drink as much as they want and hit on

           the waitresses without the waitresses complaining

   to the owners because they are the owners, but to

a pitcher of watery, overly sweet wine or a blob of green paste,

      though this'll work only if they, the owners, use a foreign

   food as the name of their emporium rather than a more

homely commodity along the line of BEAN'S, say,

        or MEATBALL'S. Yet what word is not foreign?

When I saw the phrase "animal husbandry" as a child,

          I knew what an animal was, like my basset Matilda,

    and also a husband, like my dad, who served

in this capacity to that long-suffering woman my mother,

      his wife. About that same time, kids at school

    began to tell Little Johnny Fuckerfaster jokes, which were

really the same joke over and over: the hero

        of that name would be lying on top of a girl somewhere

in the yard, and it was time for church or dinner

          or the movies, so his mother would throw open

      the back door and shout, "Little Johnny Fuckerfaster!"

and he'd shout back, "I'm fucking her as fast

as I can!" and I got it, I mean, I laughed the first ten

or twelve times I heard one of these things,

but I couldn't help wondering why, if you were a Miss Smith

or a Miss Jones and you married a Mr. Fuckerfaster,

you'd name your son Little Johnny. Ray Charles said, "I can

remember all the fuss about the Japanese bombing

Pearl Harbor, and I said, 'What the fuck is that?'

I knew there was a war in Europe, but there wasn't nobody

around to explain it." I finish up

and wash my hands and walk back to the dining room,

and the waitresses are chatting just outside the door to the kitchen,

and one says to the others, "So she says to me,

'You're a terrible friend and a horrible bitch!'" and I'm thinking,

Which is it—both? It's not bad enough

that you're a terrible friend? Just because you're a horrible bitch,

that doesn't mean you'd be a terrible friend. What if

you were a terrible friend but an excellent bitch,

a real top-shelf bitch? Somebody's got a lot of explaining to do.

Stuart Dybek

Stuart Dybek's books include *Brass Knuckles* and *I Sailed with Magellan*.
He is a professor of English at Western Michigan University.

I remember, though I might have dreamed it, a radio show I listened to when we lived on Eighteenth Street above the taxidermist. It was a program on which kids phoned the station and reported something they'd lost—a code ring, a cap gun, a ball, a doll—always their favorite. And worse than lost toys, pets, not just dogs and cats, but hamsters, parakeets, dime-store turtles with painted shells.

I'd tune to the program by accident, then forget about it, and each time I rediscovered it, it made me feel as if I were reliving the time before. The lost pets would always make me think of the old Hungarian downstairs who, people said, skinned stray cats, and of my secret pets—the foxes in his murky shop window, their glass eyes glittering fiercely from a dusty jungle of ferns and their lips retracted in a constant snarl.

D. T.

Magically, by the end of the program, everything would be found. I still don't know how they accomplished this, and recall wondering if it would work to phone in and report something that I'd always wanted as missing. For it seemed to me then that something one always wanted, but never had, was his all the same, and wasn't it lost?

MONEY FOR NOTHING

Andy Samberg

Andy Samberg is an Emmy Award–winning actor and comedian and appears regularly on *Saturday Night Live*.

In the middle of college, I transferred from UC Santa Cruz to NYU film school. I'd been working at a movie theater, and on my last day of work before I left for New York I went to the ATM next door to deposit my final piddly paycheck. When I got my receipt, I saw that I had five thousand extra dollars in my account. I was sure there'd been some kind of error, so I decided to just wait it out, assuming the bank would notice and take care of it.

I waited a couple weeks, then checked back, but the money was still in there. Since I couldn't come up with another explanation, I thought that maybe somebody in my family had deposited it as an outlandish (but welcome) gift, a congratulatory gesture for my transfer to a new school, even though that would've been totally out of character for anyone in my family. But at this point I was dying to know what the hell was going on—I mean, it was five thousand dollars out of nowhere. So I asked everyone in my family about it, and of course they all said they had no idea what I was talking about. Out of ideas, I figured it must've been a straight-up bank error, but imagined that it would probably get adjusted eventually. I certainly wasn't going to report anything, though, so I decided to just let it sit for a while.

I moved east and got settled in New York, and at some point realized that the five thousand dollars had been in my account for four months. I decided to see what would happen if I transferred out the money—maybe I'd get a call from the bank president, or have federal agents knocking at my door. I opened a new bank account at a different bank in New York, transferred the money out, and closed the old account. Here's the thing—nothing ever happened. Nobody said anything about it. So I basically found five thousand free dollars from the bank, and I used that money to fund a couple of short films I did in college at NYU. One of the films was called *Mime Comps*, a title my dad gave me. It was about a talking mime. And the other one was called *Fig and the Fairy*, which was a cautionary tale about lying. Clearly, the free money went toward some important work.

Had I lied to the bank by saying nothing? All I'd done was keep my mouth shut, like a mime. Would you have done anything different? I mean, besides spending five grand to fund a movie about a talking mime?

A couple of months later, this other thing happened, and even though it was totally unrelated, I always think of it as a bookend to the first experience. What happened was, simply, I found ten bucks floating down the sidewalk on Bleecker Street one night. At first I picked it up and was like, "Sweet! Ten dollars!" But then I looked at the bill more closely and saw that someone had written across the front of it with a marker: "YOU SUCK DICKS, GO TO HELL." I looked everywhere around me because I was so sure that someone was playing a prank and was laughing at me from the shadows, but I didn't see a soul.

Back then, taking a cab was an enormous luxury. Determined to enjoy a rare cab ride and to get rid of this foul-mouthed ten-dollar bill, I decided to flag down a taxi and unload it on a cabbie; my hope was that he might not be able to read English that well. As I'd hoped, he did not. Who knows who he ended up unknowingly passing it on to? Who knows where the five grand came from? These are mysteries that will never be solved.

SHREDS AND SHARDS

Susan Orlean

Susan Orlean is the author of *The Orchid Thief: A True Story of Beauty and Obsession* and a staff writer at *The New Yorker*.

My entire professional life has revolved around finding things. What I find are people and the stories that accompany their disparate lives. People are everywhere, of course, so it wouldn't seem that finding stories would be overly difficult. But finding that certain person—that certain story that perfectly reveals the human condition in a wholly original way—is a challenge indeed.

A tremendous number of the stories I've pursued have been sparked by some bit of random material evidence: an old sign hanging off the side of a building by a single nail, a discarded note, a flyer, an advertisement. I've always seen these seemingly useless items as crumbs left out in the world, a kind of perfect evidence of one person's existence. As a writer, and therefore an investigator, I'll follow that crumb until I reveal the story of its owner. I think the world's challenge to me is to find that found thing—the thing that isn't prepared and polished and presented to you to be consumed, the thing that feels real.

One of my favorite stories came from such a find. I was sitting on a plane, bored to tears; I'd finished the book I'd brought to read and still had hours left on my flight. I spotted the Metro section of an old *Miami Herald* that somebody had left in the seat pocket in front of me, and picked it up and began to read. Though I might not have bought this paper myself, it was the perfect way to kill time. I thought to myself, *I'll just read all the tiny stories stuck in the middle that nobody thinks are important or interesting.* And that's where I happened upon this little newspaper story about a guy stealing orchids. I was fascinated. I thought, *Wow, I can't imagine why someone would steal orchids, and even risk going to jail for it.* For the rest of the flight, I kept turning certain questions over in my head again and again: Who is this guy? Why would he steal these orchids? What's really going on here? It was all such a puzzle to me. The next thing I knew I was following the story for a couple of years.

You have to really train your eye to find the things that lead to great stories. I think it's a bit of an instinct that you either have or you don't, this curiosity for the seemingly mundane. To me, the most interesting things often seem utterly ordinary at first. The trick is to develop the habit of paying attention and poking around. I can't walk past a telephone pole with things stapled to it without stopping and reading them. Certainly your radar for finding interesting stories becomes more sensitive the more you use it, but I know I wouldn't do what I do professionally if I didn't already have a bit of an appetite for this.

Before I started working on *The Orchid Thief*, I had no interest in orchids whatsoever, no knowledge of orchids being a big business, no knowledge of orchids period. If you'd paid me a million dollars, I would never have guessed that I'd eventually do a book about orchids. It all happened because of chance and circumstance, a certain part of my brain that's always looking for the treasure in the trash. Despite what we're taught to believe, no life is a simple one. Shreds and shards you find always have the potential to open up into something bigger, and those tiny pieces that people shed along the way are enticements for finding out more about them. But you have to be aware when you're out in the world, tuned into the things that are happening all around you, truly taking notice—it's the only way you can find these bits and pieces of lives that will lead you to the grand, the triumphant, the heartbreaking, and the unexpected.

WOODSTOVE GIRL

Heidi Julavits

Heidi Julavits is a mother, journalist, novelist, and an editor of *The Believer* magazine.

The lodgings for the wedding had been prearranged for us. Guests, especially guests in their twenties, are presumed helpless when procuring shelter for themselves. Brides and grooms reason, if we don't find our friends some sort of lodging, they'll show up without a plan, crash in the country club locker room, or hook up with my lonely cousin whose primary attraction is his access to a bed. To prevent such happenings, this bride and groom had reserved us a beach house on the Connecticut shore. My boyfriend and I drove north from Brooklyn, directions in hand. From the highway, the directions wound us through some pretty woods, or woods that would have been pretty were it not November, weeks past the foliage peak, and raining. Truthfully, the day was balls-out depressing, but in an enjoyable way. It meant we could start drinking pretty much immediately. The day was thank-God-over by noon. It was a day-for-night day.

However, the houses in the certainly-pretty-under-different-circumstances woods were not particularly pretty. Most were ranches that had been subjected to destabilizing expansions, pop-top-camper second floors, and stalky porches teetering toward the trees like docks set into a lake bed that's dried up for good. Lawn ornaments saddened the situation irreparably. Perhaps this dreary scene wouldn't have impacted our mood so precipitously if we hadn't been expecting more Fitzgerald, and less Dubus senior. We'd expected to find a coastline dotted with boathouses, each a mini-version of its corresponding mansion, each mansion named with a twee-ness inversely proportionate to the grommet fortune that enabled it. Subsequently, a pall fell over my boyfriend and me. Neither of us had ever lived in the suburbs, but we'd been culturally trained to despair at the sight of them.

We were already semi-despondent by the time we pulled into the "community" or "development" or "punitive summer camp in the off-season." We were already knee-deep in the nightmarish funk that can infect you, sometimes, when you're mainlining the psychic unhappiness of a place, or that place unleashes your own psychic unhappiness on you. (We would eventually get both married to and divorced from each other, this boyfriend and I; maybe on this day I was accessing a window into this future unhappiness, though just as likely I was not.) We drove through an untended gate. The roads cul-de-saced around abandoned communal barbecue areas and picnic tables and patches of dead grass that silent-screamed, "Badminton!" like a hex. The vinyl-clad houses were arranged in the spokelike way of trailers in a trailer park. Our rental, once we found it, proved little more than a trailer. The sea was nowhere in sight.

The house's interior cemented the already glum situation. It was freezing and smelled dead-animal wonky, a smell that we attributed, optimistically, to mold. The wood-veneer walls bowed inward like wet cardboard. The doorways to the bedrooms were narrower than a narrow closet opening and privatized with stained curtains that hung only as low as our shins. Historically, decor and hygiene lapses were not enough to put me off a place. In my not-too-distant past I'd spent a few nights in a Thai beach hut where the rats ran over my mosquito netting and chewed holes in my underwear while I slept. But this place, unlike the Thai beach hut, radiated badness; some very horrible shit had gone down here. The house was speaking to us, as houses can do. It was post-traumatically stressed by the humans who had last lived in it.

The only solution was alcohol. Unfortunately, there was no alcohol. An earlier arrival had determined that the nearest liquor store was too far a drive to make it worth the trip before the first (free) wedding cocktails were served; the best he'd managed was some crappy beer from a convenience store. We cracked the crappy beers and drank them. This barely bettered things. I decided to light the woodstove to heat the place up, burn off the dampness, smoke out the dead-animal smell, reframe our disappointment as a camping adventure. I balled up some newspaper and unlatched the woodstove's door. Inside the woodstove, eerily, was a wallet-sized school photo of a smiling, ten-or-so-year-old girl. The photo was very clearly placed there, propped up by the metal grill ridges that let the fire breathe. It was in perfect shape—not burned at the edges, not torn, not even crumpled, which made the implications some-how worse.

Each of us took turns peering into the woodstove, clutching a crappy beer with greater intensity. *Don't touch it* was the general consensus. We closed the door to the woodstove, now a mini-mausoleum. We engaged in a speculative postmortem of this apparent crime scene. The girl had been killed in this house. And hacksawed into bits. And buried behind the veneer, thus explaining both the weird smell and the bowed walls. Had there been everywhere-Internet back then, we might have done some quick searches such as *missing connecticut girl ten or so italian* (the girl had brown hair and brown eyes and there were a lot of Italian businesses in the area). The Internet is fre-quently blamed for fanning hysteria and worry, but some-times it can quell it. Had we searched and found noth-ing, perhaps we would have concluded a benign self-loathing-girl fate for her; she'd really hated that school photo and had intended to burn it, then

D. J.

decided, using that perverse mind-set unique to self-loathing girls, to enshrine her bad feelings about herself.

Soon it was time to get ready for the ceremony. We dressed quickly in our shower-stall bedrooms, not wanting to be naked in the house for reasons only partially related to cold. We escaped, but not soon enough. The photo and the house infected my mood irredeemably. Doom awaited and I was its prophet. In the parking lot of the country club I spotted a childhood friend of my boyfriend's who, as an adult, had suffered a terrible accident. He'd been working on an Alaskan fishing boat and been hit in the head with a crane. His brains had spent a not-insignificant amount of time on the deck of the boat considering he survived and was basically okay, except for this side effect: He vibed as deeply evil. Once just a jealous and kind of jerky guy, postaccident he loomed around parties like a 'droid programmed to destroy specific human targets. He stared longer at you than was socially comfortable, and you could see straight through to his tampered brain that he really didn't like you, but in a super-detached, unemotional way.

During the pre-ceremony cocktails—held on a stone patio overlooking, finally, some water—I noticed him eyeballing my boyfriend more intensely than usual. As I continued to stare at him, his dark plan revealed itself to me. How obvious it was. After years of really disliking my boyfriend, he schemed to blow him away in front of all their childhood friends and family members. My boyfriend was the best man at the wedding—a bone of jealous contention with the 'droid guy, who was also very close to the groom—and in a half hour or less, my boyfriend would be standing next to the groom in a very executable position. I discerned it all in an instant—the ideal spectacle that guaranteed maximum evil-deed exposure while resonating with easy meaning. His weirder-than-usual weird behavior confirmed that I had, with my supersensitivity to doom, hacked directly into his head. Throughout the pre-ceremony cocktails, the 'droid guy returned repeatedly to the parking lot to check on something in his car trunk (obviously his shotgun). As the groom started to assemble his groomsmen, I took my boyfriend aside. You can't go up there, I said. He's going to assassinate you. I fervently broad-stroked the plan—car trunk, shotgun, ideal spectacle, etc. My boyfriend, bless him, wasn't the kind of guy to find this sort of thinking insane. He probably gave me a big, reassuring hug (one of the reasons I married him). He might have even been a bit flattered by my intricately reasoned concern, an indicator that we were both, maybe, a little too romantically daffy in the same hopeful ways. This was how much I loved him—I loved him so much that I'd imagined the perfect circumstances to have him killed.

TRASH NIGHT

Byron Case

Byron Case, wrongfully convicted of murder, is a writer serving a life sentence at Crossroads Correctional Facility in Cameron, Missouri. Visit freebyroncase.com to learn more.

I t started with a certain amount of capitalistic wishful thinking. My friends and I began combing the streets before dawn with dollar signs in our eyes, searching for salvageable curbside trash—gently used furniture, repairable appliances, still-functioning electronics. Conrad, Dave, F.C., and I were still in our early twenties, with agreeable places to live and jobs that afforded us disposable income. But the lure of free stuff was hardly beneath us. Of our usable finds, whatever none of us laid claim to was sold, usually online. Our godsend was eBay.

A simple scrapbook changed all that—turned Trash Night into an institution. We'd been hoisting a dresser into the bed of Dave's truck when a drawer rolled open. Inside was a book with pastel green pages, overflowing with photos of family get-togethers and embarrassing candid shots. Page one read, "To Joseph, for his thirteenth birthday, 1998, Love, Grandma Charles." It was a well-intentioned but totally out-of-touch keepsake. What kid wants to be reminded he was once curled up in a doggy bed, bare-assed naked (captioned "Nap time")? It wasn't surprising that little Joseph wanted to get rid of the book, and we were glad he did. It made us realize that there were incredible things being thrown away.

So this was how it worked: From the house Dave and Conrad rented, less than two miles from the hotel where I worked, the four of us would split into two teams, agreeing to meet back at the house at a certain time. We never left before midnight. Once a team got to the target neighborhood (we knew most of the city's pickup days by heart), we'd weave up and down streets at a slow, kind-of-suspicious speed, until we spotted something promising. When the car stopped, it was the passenger's job to do an EVA (Extra-Vehicular Activity) to check it out. If the pile or stack was big enough, the driver might even get out to help. In the end, back at the house, we'd put on some music and compare finds in the living room, under the glow of hundreds of white Christmas tree lights.

The four of us had had a blast doing Trash Night and the things we found were frequently amazing. But we'd roamed the streets for more than a year before we found the suitcase.

ONE NIGHT, I DROVE OVER at eleven P.M., still wearing the crisp shirt and black slacks from work. F.C. had beaten me there and was taking a nap on Conrad's gigantic brown sofa, still in his own work clothes. This was part of the routine. I walked past him and into the kitchen where Conrad and Dave were cooking a late dinner of ramen noodles. We had a few beers, shared a few jokes. Eventually F.C. staggered in with pillow creases on his face and the conversation turned to trash.

"Northeast's pickup's in the morning, guys," he said.

"Forget that, man," said Dave. "It's all junk up there."

The northeastern part of the city wasn't the most promising for our kind of trash. Decades ago, the homes there were nice, but over the years it had become a haven for gangbangers and paranoid druggies. But F.C. was persistent. "Hey, Northeast's where we found those board games. And that one box of pictures. There's some good stuff up there."

After a while, Dave agreed to go. "But if we're taking the truck," he insisted, "somebody's buying me gas."

THE **FIRST** **SIGNS** **OF** **TRASH** that night were a stained orange mattress and some black thirty-gallon bags. Conrad steered his '67 Oldsmobile monstrosity onto an east-west street; I opened a new pack of cigarettes. We passed mounds of garbage: shadeless lamps, totaled easy chairs, broken bed frames. A lot of what we saw was bags—kitchen trash, most likely. Untouchable. Then, up ahead, Conrad spotted a three-drawer filing cabinet on his side of the street. He slowly applied the brakes. "Uh-oh."

"I'm on it," I said. I'd seen the cabinet right away. My seat belt was already off, my door unlatched. I was on the curb before the big block even started idling.

But all the drawers were empty, so we moved on.

Our first score came a few blocks over, where we found an old typewriter set on a small wooden crate. The typewriter was broken and uninteresting; in the crate, though, were some vinyl 33s with titles like *Connie Francis Sings Jewish Favorites*. They'd do nicely padding out our presentation later.

Next we checked a broken steamer trunk full of children's costumes. Then a box of high school textbooks. Then some paper bags full of random doodads, including crude wooden models of old ships. The mounted deer head with a missing antler seemed like a keeper, even if the other things didn't, and when I opened two boxes of frighteningly over-sharpened butcher's knives with THE KNIFE MAN written on the flaps, I knew we were on our way to an impressive little trove.

When we hadn't passed anything worth stopping for in nearly twenty minutes, I was feeling less optimistic. "I don't know, Dave was probably right," I said. "Northeast sucks."

"We're going to find something good eventually," said Conrad, taking another corner. Ahead was nothing but a rusted water heater and a bluish suitcase. "Okay, you ready?"

"For that? Forget it—it's nothing."

"Come on, we've gotta look." His fingers were drumming on the steering wheel. I was ready to call it a night. All I had to do, I thought, was show him the thing was empty and we could be on our way.

It wasn't empty.

Small and made of cloth, the case was patterned with embroidered vines and ugly flowers. It had a surprising weight when I lifted it to my knee. The zipper opened without a struggle, and I couldn't hide my surprise when I looked inside and saw exactly the sort of contents that Trash Night had come to be about.

Conrad noticed from the car. "We got something?"

I just smiled and closed the lid.

W ITH EVERYTHING LAID OUT ON the living room floor, we all sat in a semicircle around the collected booty. Beers had been opened and the room was hazy with smoke. Dave and F.C. had shown off their so-so finds—some hefty catalogs of sex toys, an ugly painting of a fantasy scene, some Herb Alpert records, a toy piano, and a box containing nothing but unread paperbacks by Stephen King—and Conrad and I were showing ours. The deer head earned a place of honor above our front door and the records were appreciated in an ironic way. Our creepy knives were a mild curiosity. The suitcase, though, saved for last, was our pièce de résistance.

We opened the case. On top were a couple of framed portraits, which we stood on either side of the case. One was a photo from a school dance, maybe a prom, showing a thick-bodied Latina in a black dress. She stood alone between two draping floral arrangements and her smile looked rehearsed. The other picture was of a young marine, also Latino, with a narrow, cleft chin. Dave snickered at the girl's photograph. "Oh, this'll be a hoot!"

F.C. reached into the suitcase and pulled out a horse miniature—one of those dainty porcelain knickknacks practically every preteen American girl adorns her shelves with. He pranced it across the coffee table and whinnied as he left it to feed at the trough of a brimming ashtray. Out came a box of cheap jewelry followed by a shoe box bulging with notes and washed-out snapshots. Under these were a plush frog, some generic vanilla perfume, high school yearbooks, a couple of supermarket romance novels, and other super-girly trinkets. All of it, straight through to the diaries down at the bottom, was fodder for our sophomoric commentary.

Ineffectual diary locks were easily pried open with F.C.'s bottle opener. While I went thumbing through one of the yearbooks, F.C. and Dave started reading entries out loud. The first few entries were innocent enough, even a little funny for their run-on sentences and iffy grammar. The author was Jennifer (we got that much from the embossed yearbooks), a pretty average high school senior, it seemed. Until we read about the problems at home.

The uncle she lived with had caught her making out with her boyfriend on the back porch one night. After running the boyfriend off at gunpoint, she wrote, he dragged her into the house, screaming obscenities, and proceeded to beat her "for kissing on a boy." We tried to dismiss the incident. We told each other that the uncle was just a disciplinarian, that it was a cultural thing—what did we know?—but these justifications became difficult as we read on. The uncle was an alcoholic, abusive to both Jennifer and his wife. The diaries were full of incidents like the one from the back porch, some brief, others covering multiple pages.

A knot grew in my stomach. Sometimes it was obvious why something had been thrown away. In this case, it wasn't—so many personal treasures tossed to the curb at once, and with such awful things going on in the owner's life. This tossed suitcase implied bad things, and I wasn't the only one to pick up on it.

Looking up from some pictures, Conrad asked, "When did she write in there last?"

The most recent entry was about four months old. Leafing back a few pages, F.C. found where Jennifer had written about hurting her ankle on the stairs. The uncle again. She wrote that he didn't know about the baby, that she was scared of what he might do if he found out. Someone called "L"—most likely her boyfriend, the father of her unborn kid—wanted to run away with her to Dallas. He had family they could stay with there. He said he wanted to give her and their baby the best possible life. But, she wrote, sometimes she wasn't sure she wanted to be alive at all.

I sank back into the couch cushions. Dave took a long, contemplative swig of his beer. Something had to happen for her stuff to be thrown out in a suitcase. But nobody had any idea what, if anything, could be done about it. So we drank. Gradually, concern for Jennifer's fate was lessened by the alcohol. It became easy to imagine that she was fine, living happily ever after with L in sunny Texas, far away from her evil uncle. Maybe the uncle suffered sudden liver failure, kicking the bucket and leaving everything to his long-suffering wife and niece. Maybe after the funeral, Jennifer threw away all the reminders of her painful teenage years—the diaries, all the Polaroids and girly bric-a-brac— as sort of cathartic, growing-up thing. Maybe, with the uncle gone, L could move in with Jennifer and her aunt to help raise the baby and pay bills. Maybe, I thought, everything ends hunky-dory.

A SIDE FROM F.C.'S SNORES, THE house was quiet when I woke up groggy the next morning. Our found treasures covered the floor, and Jennifer's pictures were splayed out over the coffee table, alongside ashtrays and empty bottles. I sat for a few minutes, rubbing my eyes, trying to collect myself without thinking too much about the revelations of the night before.

Without knowing exactly why, I picked up a couple of the pictures. In one, Jennifer was smooshing a puppy against her cheek and grinning hugely. I slipped it into my pocket before standing, then walked as quietly as the fussy floorboards would allow to the front door, and outside to my car. It was blindingly bright.

Trash Night was over.

AMMONITE

Billy Bragg

Billy Bragg, a singer and songwriter for over thirty years, blends elements of folk music, punk rock, and protest songs. His latest album is called *Mr. Love & Justice*.

Through the garden, down the steps, and there I am on the beach. Before I lived here, on the southwest coast of England, I thought the beach was always the same, always constant. But I've learned that every day the sea is different, and every day the beach is different. Some days the sea churns and other days it's flat and laps at the shore. Some days the tide runs up the beach and chases you, other days the tide is so low you can play a game of football. The shape of the beach changes, the width changes. There're different stones, new sand, fresh ropes of seaweed. In the space of a day, the whole thing gets swallowed whole and spit back up, all turned around.

Because of the constant change, the beach is a great place to find things. Flotsam and jetsam wash up all the time, things torn off of boats. After big storms, bits of trees wash up onshore, even gigantic trunks of trees, scorched black from a lightning strike. You sometimes find animals washed up, too— birds, fish, jellyfish. Even in death, they're breathtaking reminders of nature's strange beauty.

But the fossils are what really stop me and cause me to contemplate. Each day, I walk with my dog along the beach at the base of a towering cliff, and I rarely look out at the ocean or the sky—I'm paying closer attention to the millions and millions of pebbles under my feet, these tiny little rocks. And then I'll spot something buried deep in the pebbles, a natural curve: the fossil remains of a little spiral-shelled animal called an ammonite. Once you've found one, you're always looking for that curve, that hint of a curve, that whorled shell fused to a rock; certain of these rocks, on their undersides, reveal the ammonite's crystallized internal workings. You come to understand that you're the first person who's touched this rock in 150 million years. Perhaps you stick the rock in your pocket. You feel a sense of awe as you walk around, unconsciously running your thumb and forefinger over its smoothness and curve, and you think, *This was once alive. It was once a living thing.*

You'll find a fossilized bivalve seashell embedded in a piece of stone, and it's 170 million years old, and next to it, a hundred yards away, you might find a shell from a bivalve that died yesterday. It gives you the sense that things change, but also remain the same. These animals were living and dying here millions of years ago, and they're still here today going through the same cycle. Although your time here may be fleeting, there's an underlying permanence.

If only I could understand time, things would be so much easier. Those things that I love doing wouldn't whiz by, and those things that I hate doing would pass quickly. I'm always trying to get a better handle on time. Time absolutely confounds me. Where's the week gone, where's the year gone? I always feel I haven't done the shit that I really needed to do. The fossils, though, they're a reminder that certain things happen over much greater spans of time. The same animals still wash ashore millions of years later. Not everything is transient. Some things persist. Not everything is swept away. The cliff, packed with ancient ammonites, slowly crumbles its stones down, and the sea takes its time with them and then leaves them for you to find. If you don't find any fossils one day, the tide will come in and turn the stones upside down, and you'll find them the next time you look.

ALL GOOD DEEDS
MUST BE PUNISHED

Patton Oswalt

Patton Oswalt, a comedian based in Los Angeles, is known for his work on stage and on screen, including the film *Ratatouille*.

Years ago, I was driving along in Sherman Oaks, minding my own business, when I happened to spot something strange in the road. I pulled over next to it, opened my door, and was surprised to find a fat brown leather wallet sitting on the asphalt. I was puzzled. Wallets belong in pockets and purses, not on roads. So I scooped up this lost wallet and drove away, nothing but the best of intentions in my heart. I was going to make somebody's day, I imagined; someone had lost his or her beloved wallet and would be thrilled to hear that I'd come to the rescue.

After a few minutes, I pulled up in front of my house and began to examine what I'd found. When I opened the wallet, a face stared back at me from a faded driver's license; a man's face, with dark eyes, dark hair, and a bushy mustache. Being the respectful person that I am, I didn't want to go rifling through the wallet looking for a number. Instead, I went inside, looked up the man's name in the phone book, and gave him a call. Boy, was he ever going to be happy to hear from me!

"Hello?" a gruff voice answered. He sounded vaguely Yugoslavian, but I couldn't exactly place the accent.

"Hi," I said. "You don't know me but I found your wallet—"

"You shouldn't have my wallet," he interrupted.

"Yes. Yes, I know. I found it. In Sherman Oaks. I don't know if you live in Sherman Oaks, but that's where it was. I want to return it to you."

"Oh," he said. "Okay. I'll tell you where I live and you can come give it to me."

Now, I'm a generous man, but this request was a little too much. And I told him so. "Well, really you should come get it from me. I mean, I found it and everything."

"Why do you have my wallet?" the man bellowed. *"Bring it here!"*

Me? The Noble Finder? Drive to *his* house? It just didn't make sense. My whole Good Samaritan plan was really taking a nosedive. And why was the guy so angry with me? If I'd stolen his wallet, would I really be going through all this trouble and abuse to return it to him? I was losing patience fast, but managed to remain calm, and was eventually able to convince him to pick up his wallet from my house.

When he arrived, he lingered at the edge of my front porch. I invited him inside and he shook his head.

"Give me the wallet," he said, slowly and evenly. It was the same tone you might use to talk a gun out of a criminal's hand, or convince someone not to jump off a five-story building. He seemed to suspect me of playing some strange, twisted game where I'd invite him into my home and then refuse to give him his wallet. I couldn't tell if he was an asshole or simply a bit culturally dim, which is what kept me from socking him in the nose.

I just wanted the whole ordeal to be over. I stepped out on the porch and handed him his wallet. He didn't thank me, but gave me a look like, "I hope you've learned your lesson."

I did. Next time I find a wallet, I'll keep the damn thing.

R-O-C-K O-N

Marlon Hill

Marlon Hill, profiled in the Stefan Fatsis book *Word Freak*, is a nationally ranked Scrabble champion who lives in Baltimore.

Twelve years ago, I took the train from Baltimore to Dallas to play in the National Scrabble Championship. I'm often ranked as one the best players in the country, but everyone agrees that I've got the worst luck of anybody in the scene. If you stick your hand in the bag and draw two tiles, two tiles only, the worst two tiles you can draw are W and U. I draw these all the time! In too many tournaments to count, unlucky draws have sunk my battleship.

That day, when I arrived at the train station in Dallas, near Reunion Arena, and stepped off the train, I noticed at my feet a perfectly round rock. Its smooth, unblemished shape made it stand out from all the other rocks along the tracks, so I picked it up and dropped it into my pocket, hoping it might bring me a change of luck. Well, I came in second at Nationals that weekend and won ten thousand dollars. Ever since, the rock has brought me luck. Sometimes friends have given me little toys and trinkets that are meant to bring me good luck in Scrabble, but something about the fact that I found that rock on the ground seems to make its luck more pure. It came to me serendipitously, and smiles fortune upon me whenever I need a lucky break the most.

Weirdly, I often forget to bring the rock with me when I leave Baltimore to play in tournaments. Every time I lose, I say, "I wish I had that goddamn rock!"

B. R.

DEAR THE ROCK

Kimya Dawson

Kimya Dawson is a singer-songwriter living in Olympia, Washington. Her solo albums include *My Cute Fiend Sweet Princess* and *Remember That I Love You*; her first children's album is called *Alphabutt*.

One of my first finds, when I was like five years old, was my neighbor's glass eye. That was pretty scary. He was this older kid who lived up the street named Jimmy McKinstry—kind of a Dungeon Master–y, pre–Trenchcoat Mafia Trenchcoat Mafia type of kid. Jimmy McKinstry always wore his black trenchcoat, and had long, greasy hair. He and another kid in the neighborhood had been playing in the street with BB guns, and naturally he got shot in the eye and lost his eye.

Growing up, my brother and I used to put on these mini-carnivals in our backyard all the time. We'd charge kids a penny to throw a rock through a tire to win a prize; if they won we'd give out pine cones or popcorn or paper airplanes. Jimmy McKinstry must've been looking in our money can, and I guess his eye fell out, but he didn't see where it went. Later, I was counting money and I found his eye. I remember shouting, *"There's an eyeball in the pennies!"* And Jimmy came rushing over—like, "Damn, there it is!"—and stared at me accusingly with his gaping socket.

I'VE ALWAYS BEEN KIND OF obsessed with pictures of people I don't know. Families. Kids. Old men. I used to work in the library in my town. Part of my reason for wanting to work there was all the years and years of archived yearbooks. I would just be like, "Yeah, I'm gonna go organize this back room, guys, gotta shelve some books," and then I'd sit and look through old yearbooks for hours, year by year, seeing how people had aged over the years. I've always had this obsession with getting glimpses of people I don't know and trying to imagine their stories. That's why I love finding pictures. I love absorbing the expressions on people's faces—they're totally caught in that moment. Once, I plucked a Polaroid off the sidewalk of a fat kid in a tight T-shirt flexing his muscles; that was one of my favorite pictures I ever found. He was just so *happy*; he was like, "Whoa-*ohhhh*—look at my biceps!"

Especially in candid pictures of people, something rare and poignant's often captured. They were just sitting there thinking about something, and someone caught 'em in the act. It's sort of the same as peeking in someone's window when you're walking along the sidewalk—and we all do that, too . . . right?

I THINK THE CENTERPIECE OF my collection is a really great find that was gifted to me. A friend of mine found this big manila envelope full of photocopied letters that fourth- and fifth-graders had written to The Rock. The wrestler. It was amazing, these city kids pouring their hearts out to him about why he's their hero. "Dear The Rock, you inspire me. . . ." I'm always wondering: Did The Rock write back?

It was like a class project—the whole class wrote letters to The Rock. Some of them were just like, "Hey The Rock, you're so strong! I think it's really cool that you kick butt." And some of them were like, "I don't have a dad. I wish you were my dad. You seem really nice. And I want someone like you to take care of me." These really anguished ones and then ones like, "Oh, that match you had against Stone Cold Steve Austin was so cool." Sometimes both hues in the same letter. "I want you to be my dad because you kick ass, and I don't have a dad."

Discovering letters like these is really like finding treasure—a special kind of treasure. The notes can make you sad, but they're also really exciting. It's almost like you're inside another person, seeing through their eyes for a minute. It's one of the most exciting feelings in life. I guess some people think it's too voyeuristic to read other people's letters—that it's just plain wrong—but I don't think it is. It would be wrong if there was an address and a phone number, and I called the person and was like, "Ooooh, I can't believe you said this." If I tried to get involved. But I think just reading something a stranger wrote and dropped is okay.

It's tough, though, 'cause I've written really awkward diaries myself. Now I journal everything online and I have no shame, but there's journals from when I was sixteen that I wouldn't want anyone to see. I used to write love letters to Sting. I filled entire journals with letters to Sting. Sting was my The Rock. There's one letter I wrote to him, it's the only thing I've written in my life that I'm not comfortable sharing with the world. Maybe someday. But whenever I think of this one particular letter and poem I wrote to Sting, I feel really, really uncomfortable. If someone found that, I might die. It's a good reminder to me to be sensitive when I'm reading other people's stuff—to be sure I'm laughing along with them, and not laughing *at* them.

Photo courtesy of Frank Warren

POST-ROCK

Frank Warren

Frank Warren founded PostSecret, an ongoing community mail art project in which people send him their anonymous secrets on one side of a homemade postcard.

My daughter's name is Hailey. She's thirteen years old. When Hailey was very young, we started to go for walks out in nature. We'd climb a hill, we'd walk around a lake. But we especially loved to walk through creeks; we have a lot of natural creeks here in Germantown, Maryland. Once or twice a month in the summertime, we'd drive out to these creeks and go wading out into the water. We had these old sneakers we'd wear so we could let the water run over our feet and ankles. Hailey and I would look for tadpoles and watch the leaves float down the creek. We'd observe things—the trees, the birds, the sounds— and we'd peer into the water and check out the stones and rocks. Hailey would sometimes pick up something from our walks and bring it home. Usually it was a rock, but sometimes she would pick up a little piece of a broken shell or a leaf—souvenirs from our time out there together.

One day I got an idea. I went online and found a place that engraves stones. The company will take a natural stone of their choice and engrave it for you—whatever message you like. I thought it would be great to have one of those online places engrave a message on a stone for Hailey, or even just her name, and then I could take that stone and plant it in the creek where we'd be walking. With a little gentle guidance, I figured, Hailey would discover this stone, and it might be a neat thing for her to wonder about, a serendipitous treasure.

The engraved rocks were about the size of a child's shoe, and weighed maybe ten pounds. Because of their size and color they looked unusual among the indigenous creek rocks, odd enough to pique one's curiosity. In one rock, JUST SHOW UP was carved on one side and on the other side it said HAILEY; another was engraved TRY, TRY, TRY and the back said HAILEY; a third said DON'T DREAM and the reverse read PREPARE.

I did this about once a year, each summer, starting when she was four or five. Early on, it felt a bit like a Santa Claus type of thing—a little white lie was involved, but on a deeper level I really felt like we were sharing something special, that I was creating this wonderful memory that might have meaning for her that would live on in ways that I couldn't even imagine.

From the beginning, Hailey used to get very emotional. One summer she found the engraved stone I'd planted and started crying, overwhelmed by how magical it was that she'd found this stone with a special little phrase on it and also her name. I came home and told the story to my wife, and she said, "Okay, you've got to stop this." I had to lobby my wife to let me continue with the stones. I said, "No, no. It's really something special; it's like a tradition for us." She reluctantly gave her consent, even though Hailey's reactions were always so strong. Year after year, we'd go back to the creek and I'd watch happily as Hailey discovered her special stones.

The last time we went to the creek, Hailey was ten years old. I'd had one of the stones made and hidden it in the rushing water of a beautiful creek in Glen Echo Park, which was an amusement park at the turn of the century and is now home to artists' huts, a carousel, and a museum. As we were walking over a bridge toward the creek, I noticed that there were dozens of kids playing in the creek bed. They were part of some kind of summer-camp outing, and it was a hive of activity: campers, counselors, parents, all picnicking and running around. I thought to myself, *Oh, man, what do I do?* At first I figured we could just come back another time, but then I thought about how likely it was that one of these kids would discover the stone and take it. Only one thing to do—

go down there among the crowd of kids, shepherd Hailey toward the stone's general vicinity, and let her discover it.

We headed down and waded into the creek. There were kids all around, splashing, shouting, playing war games, and I was trying to guide Hailey through them to where her stone was. We got close to it, and sure enough, she found it and was as excited as ever. She pulled the stone up out of the water and cried, "Look, Dad, look! It's a rock; it's got a message on it!" At this point she'd gotten the rest of the kids' attention. Soon all the campers were coming over, counselors were coming around, and even the parents were interested. Hailey was looking at the rock, showing it around, and the other kids were looking at her in amazement. Parents were looking at her, at me, and at the stone, and there was this look of childlike wonder in their eyes. Before long, all of the kids began searching for more stones like Hailey's.

Then Hailey, newly thrilled, burst out, "Dad, it's got my *name* on the other side!" When she said this, the awe of the campers doubled. Instantly, though, I started getting these knowing looks from the counselors and the parents that said, "Oh, okay, *now* we get it. You planted the stone there." They seemed almost wistful. For better or for worse, the world made sense to them again. The mystery was gone.

Hailey has yet to find out the truth behind her magic stones. It's kind of like the Santa Claus story—you don't know when that point is when your child realizes there is no Santa, but you're certainly not going to be the one to tell them. For now, the stones are this special thing that she and I shared and continue to share even to this day.

I JUST CRUSH A LOT

Nick Paumgarten

Nick Paumgarten is a writer and editor at *The New Yorker*.

"Look at this thing! It was in the middle of the street!"

Some people bring flowers home to their loved ones; my wife, who was my girlfriend at the time, had brought me an old, flattened aluminum bucket that she and her roommate had found. I loved it.

I've always been mesmerized by industrial ruins, whether it's decaying buildings, old machinery—big hunks of rusted metal—or just little rusted bolts. Too often, you'll come across something really cool, but you can't move it because it's too heavy and gigantic. If you're in the ruined part of an old industrial city, you might discover, say, a 1940s oil truck, and it will have become almost like this piece of the Earth, an unmovable boulder. I'll pluck up tiny, old metal parts and pocket them as souvenirs of the larger pieces I couldn't bring home.

The flattened bucket was gorgeous; it was spotted with rust and hardened dirt and must have met a steamroller that didn't like the cut of its jib. My wife liked it as much as I did. She's an artist and had the idea of making more buckets just like it. At the hardware store, though, she had trouble making herself understood to some of the sales clerks.

She'd hold up a metal bucket. "Will this one crush well?" she'd ask.

"No, no," the clerk would quickly assure her. "That one won't crush at all."

"Well then," she'd say, "that's not the one I want—I want the one that will crush well!"

She tried a slew of different buckets: dropped things on them, even ran them over with the car, but she could never reproduce the found bucket. As it turns out, it's nearly impossible to re-create the forces of time and chance. But at least we've still got the original bucket. To this day, it's hanging on the wall in my office.

Illustration by Dan Tice, based on a photo found by Allison Clarke, Lafayette, LA

D. T.

Michelle Quint

Michelle Quint is a managing editor at *McSweeney's* and writes for
Paste Magazine and the *San Francisco Chronicle*.

It was the following Monday when Kevin Bass gave Lee the picture. And in that moment Lee knew just one truth, clear as he had ever known anything.

"Check it out, man," Kevin had said, handing him the photo and giving his left arm a punch. "They'd fuck for sure." Three people filled the 4" × 6" square, but only Lee faced forward. On his left and right were two identical profiles, flipped images in a mirror. The Potter twins loved having their picture taken, especially together.

The photo had been taken at the party. That Friday had marked the first Mardi Gras after the storm and they'd all resolved to do it up right. Jennifer's mom had agreed to a small get-together and even bought them a few bottles of rum for the occasion. But word spread, as it always did, and the party quickly swelled past her control. Lee had spent all of Saturday trying to recall the previous night, but the haze of his hangover had left him pleasantly dull. And so he'd resigned to leave the night shrouded in fog, vaguely hoping he hadn't acted too much a fool. Now, staring at the picture, he tried anew to recall.

He clearly remembered arriving too early. For a while, he'd made awkward conversation with Jennifer and her mom in the living room, where he'd downed three warm beers in quick succession. More people arrived. They had mixed Hurricanes in a Radio Flyer. Someone had fallen and bled on the carpet. Then things began to blur and conflate.

Lee scrutinized the picture, hoping to further jog something, to place himself there. He both remembered this moment and did not, like watching a forgotten childhood movie. The picture cut him off at his hairline, making his long, oval face look even longer. His dark eyes were fixed firrmly ahead; his lips curved up at their corners. Invisible arms wrapped around each girl in a U, drawing them close, his left hand unnaturally large in the foreground, gripping a small shoulder.

Pressed hotly against him on either side were the twins, their necks heavy with metallic Mardi Gras beads (though he noticed Liz had fewer strands than Carrie, a point of contention he was sure). On his left, Liz had puckered her lips against his cheek, her neck extending gracefully, showcasing a perfect jawline. But against his other cheek, Carrie merely smiled dreamily, lips closed, so that her nose received the impact of his cheekbone and smashed down in a hook; an old woman's nose. Both the girls' eyes were closed gently, lovely lashes swept upward. In the photo, the threesome stood slightly off-center, to the left, leaving a triangular black void over Carrie's shoulder, where the party must have pulsed behind them. The blackness was disturbed only by a small dot of white light. Lee searched it for meaning but found none.

But now other things were coming back. He remembered trying to mount a skateboard and falling. *He* had bled on the carpet. Jennifer had caught him on all fours, trying to rub out the stain with some beer and his sweatshirt. He remembered belting "Living on a Prayer" into the night with Scott and Kevin, the crushing joy he felt then. And the solemn ceremony when they'd poured their sticky pink drinks onto the grass, in memory of those who'd drowned in the floodwaters.

And now, creeping into his consciousness like a noxious gas, a new memory. A small, damp hand grabbing his own, leading him—two bodies crashing together, stumbling away from the party. He saw the shed, the thin metal door ajar. He remembered cocking one eye shut, trying to steady the image of the girl in the darkness, and thinking that he'd had no idea that Carrie liked him like that. Wet, careless kisses on his neck, her hand leading his to cup her small breast. Her free hand struggling with his belt buckle. Christ. His stomach lurched as her face materialized in his memory; her quizzical look at finding him soft; the jerky, painful grips that followed. Then all was confusion and light and noise and Jennifer's mom was yelling, "Elizabeth Potter!" and yanking her up off her knees and out of the shed. Then it was only him in the dark, prostrate and alone.

He looked up from the photo. Kevin was still grinning maniacally, shifting his weight from foot to foot in a strange little dance. Lee couldn't remember how he'd gotten home that night, if he'd gotten a ride or simply walked. But his memory of the shed, now exhumed and dusted off, was achingly acute. Of course, he thought distantly, he could blame the turn of events on any number of things—the liquor, the start from Jennifer's mom. But as he looked back to his face in the picture and met his own dark stare, the eyes so sure and clear, yet, yet . . . Yes, unmistakably searching beyond the lens. And then, in a buckling instant, he knew one thing for certain, as clear as anything he'd ever known. He did not want either of the Potter twins, or anyone like them. He wanted Kevin Bass, who'd been holding the camera.

MESSAGE IN 1,000 BOTTLES

Tad Friend

Tad Friend is a staff writer for *The New Yorker* and the author of *Lost in Mongolia: Travels in Hollywood and Other Foreign Lands.*

Seven years ago, my wife and I moved into a brownstone apartment in Brooklyn. Roughly three times a week, I'd find a white or green plastic bag filled with bottles that someone had hung over the black fence in front of our building during the night. The bottles were a weird mix of upmarket soft drinks, like Schweppes ginger ale, Perrier sparkling water, and cranberry juice, and a lot of down-market beer—middle-American brews you don't really see in Brooklyn, like Schaefer and Piel's. They'd leave the bottles dangling there and I'd take them out and add them to our recycling bin. It was sort of odd, though, because there was this whole long street, and no other bags were left on anyone else's fence. If the person who was leaving the bottles lived on our street they would have their own recycling bin, and if they didn't live on the street, then why were they picking *our* building?

There are four apartments in the building, and for some reason I'm the only one who pays attention to the appearance of these bottles—nobody else bothers taking down the bag or even seems to notice. So I put the bag's contents in our recycling, feeling slightly put-upon, and wonder what the deal is.

This has gone on for nearly seven years now, and I've never figured out who's leaving the bottles.

Late one night, my wife was looking out the window and saw an elderly couple shuffling up the street. When they reached our building, they lifted the bag off the fence, so she called down, "Hey, do you know who leaves that bag?" The couple put the bag back and ran off at top speed without looking up; they must have thought she was shouting at them not to take the bottles. My wife said it was almost as though our fence was a part of their regular route—maybe they stop sometimes and take down the bag, which would explain why many nights there's no bag there. But this still doesn't explain who's leaving the bottles.

Three or sometimes four times a week, a new bag appears. It's fascinating to me that someone is generating so many bottles in such constant rhythm. The bags are always hung with a certain amount of care, and it's not like there are twelve bottles inside and an alcoholic is hiding them from his wife. For the life of me, I don't know what the fuck is going on. The weirdest part is that I've left the bag there to see what happens, and the mystery person always waits until I've taken down the bag before he or she adds another. There's an element of cat and mouse to it. Even when we leave town for a week or more, we will return home to a single bag on the fence, never an accumulation. I imagine that while we're gone, the person is sadly disappointed to see that I haven't been keeping up with my job of taking the bag off the fence.

You would think that after all this time we'd have discovered the culprit. You come home often enough and at weird hours, you're bound to catch someone in the act, just once. The closest thing to a Neighborhood Watch we have is this guy in a long overcoat who's always smoking a cigar and moving his arms up and down the sidewalk, wrapped in his own thoughts. My wife has gotten to know him a little bit, and she's asked him, "Have you seen this person who leaves the bags?" And he says, "No." He's out there day and night, and even he has never seen anyone. Sometimes I've wondered if he could be the culprit; I haven't dusted for prints or anything, but I've never seen him drinking soft drinks or beer out there, and so I've gradually decided that it's probably not him. I feel like somewhere there's someone with a pair of binoculars carefully assessing the situation, waiting to make a countermove.

These kinds of visitations can make your thinking a little batty. It's like the bottles are being placed there not by a person at all but by a mischievous universal force. And a part of me enjoys preserving the mystery. If it turned out there was some mundane explanation, like the super next door has a couple of drinks on the job and then when he leaves at four A.M. hangs the bag over our fence because it's easier than going downstairs to the basement on the way out, it would be a little disappointing. In a way, I appreciate the shoemaker's-elves quality of the mystery.

Taking the bag down on my to work is annoying, but I'll admit, there's something delightful about it, too. I'll walk out the front door, monotonous things on my mind, and then I find the bag, and it's a little tinderbox for my brain. There's a spark of annoyance and at the same time a sense of something out there I can't fully understand. It's kind of like those old rail-yard switches, the levers that switch the trains from one track to another. The bag on the fence is my lever—it galvanizes some secret part of my brain that needs to be fucked with. The anonymity of it amuses and intrigues me. There's a strange pleasure in the appearance of each new bag—it's like a Rorschach inkblot, where you can read into it what you like. If there was a little note attached to the bag saying, *I'm Bob; we don't have a recycling bin. Can you please recycle these?* then that would be the end of it. You would probably answer him, *Dear Bob, no,* or, *Dear Bob, okay,* and that would be the end of it. But the idea that there's an inscrutable message in these thousands of bottles—left without a return address, written in some gnomic and invisible language you can't understand—is what enables you to dream.

TAKE THE FROG

Eli Horowitz

**Eli Horowitz is the managing editor and publisher of *McSweeney's*
and editor of *The People of Paper*, among other books.**

One day in kindergarten, my class took a field trip to the beach. "The beach" just meant a small patch of sand next to Lake Accotink, in northern Virginia. But this was still as exciting as you'd imagine, and we all spent a few blissful hours dipping our toes in the water and building sand castles. The high point came when one of us found a small frog—I think we assumed it was a baby frog, but it might just have been malnourished or deformed, or simply a diminutive species. In any case, this frog appeared, and the next two hours were spent building frog castles, frog pools, frog waterslides. Great fun was had by all—frog included, surely.

Eventually the sky darkened and we were herded toward the bus. Everyone said their sad good-byes to our amphibian friend. I must have been one of the last to leave, because somehow, instead of bidding farewell to the young/malnourished/shrimpy frog, I sneaked him into my hand and scurried onto the bus. I just wasn't ready to let go. I sat there in my seat, frog clenched in my fist. I must not have been too subtle, because I remember someone asking, "What are you holding there?" "Um, sand," I cleverly replied. Somehow that explanation was sufficient.

Over the next twenty minutes, I gradually realized the magnitude of my actions. What initially felt like courageous ingenuity—"Instead of *leaving* the frog, I can *take* the frog!"—began to seem less wise. It occurred to me that the authority figures might not share my excitement. It also occurred to me that frogs might not thrive in the ecosystem of my clenched fist. My pride curdled into concern, and then shame and fear. No one seemed to doubt my sand-hand story, but the fact remained that I was sitting on a school bus with forbidden wildlife suffocating in my sweaty paw. I just wanted the whole episode to be over. The frog, squirmy at first, now appeared to be napping.

We finally pulled up to the school and filed off the bus. As we walked toward the front door, I looked left and chucked the contents of my hand to the right, toward some tall grass. Tall grass! Frogs like tall grass, right? He'd live a long and happy life, right? I kept my eyes focused on the big red doors of the school, afraid to look back and see, stuck atop the weeds, a tiny green corpse staring at me with milky, accusing eyes.

Some finders are not ready for the responsibility, and some finds are better left unfound. Some finds should remain where they belong, next to Lake Accotink, young and free, hopping alone among crumbling sand castles in the cool Virginian dusk.

ONE THAT GOT AWAY

Robert Evans

Robert Evans has produced eighteen movies, including *The Godfather*, *Chinatown*, *Rosemary's Baby*, and *Love Story*. He is also the author of a memoir, *The Kid Stays in the Picture*.

It was 1991. I'd been working on my book, *The Kid Stays in the Picture*, for three years, but couldn't finish it. I knew I needed to find peace of mind, and to find peace of mind, I knew I had to go somewhere far from civilization where I could be completely undisturbed. I knew I needed to go alone.

I flew to Maui and stayed in a tiny cottage right on the ocean. When I got there, I had thirty calls I had to make. Within a week, I didn't even know what a telephone was. I spent my days at a writing desk, listening to the sounds of rain in the afternoon, the wind at night. In the mornings, I'd walk a mile or two along the beach, knee-deep in the water, and never see another soul. Just the sand, water, and sky, all filled with a quality of light that was so dazzling, so stunning, I felt like a man born blind who'd one day, without warning, been granted sight. I'd talk to the gulls. I'd talk to myself. I was as alone as I'd ever been, but I wasn't lonely. I was where I needed to be.

The water was so clear that you could be fifty yards out, waist deep, and see every shell on the bottom. I plucked flat skipping stones from under my feet and skimmed them across the lagoon. I watched fish slalom between my legs. Lobsters scooted past. These lobsters, they captivated me. Some distance down the beach from my cabin, I'd discovered a forgotten old grill atop a metal drum, and I became determined to catch a lobster and grill it right there on the sand. I pieced a net together and brought it on my walks, casually—*I wasn't hunting for lobsters*, I told myself, *I was just walking and happened to have a net*.

Lobsters are tricky, though. They make themselves hard to find, and then when you find a lobster, they're so damn quick—I could never quite catch them. Finally, two weeks in, I snared one. Thrilled, I lifted the net high above my head and splashed toward shore. Once I was up on dry land, I pulled the lobster from the net and held it in front of my face to examine it in the morning light. Suddenly, out of nowhere, a pelican swooped down with a single barked cry, snatched the lobster from me, and sailed away wordlessly, gliding out of sight into a grove of Norfolk pines. It was a violent, jarring heist—the damn thing had almost taken my head off. For a moment, I just stood there, stunned, amazed, and then I began to laugh. I laughed the laughter you laugh when there's nobody around for miles to catch you laughing. A revelation blasted me—in my life back home, I'd been so afraid of the unexpected that avoiding it had become a constant battle. But the unexpected, I understood all at once, couldn't harm me. The unpredictable was to be embraced, not shuttered. I felt a rush, a freedom I'd never known. I felt released. I'd found my motherfucking peace of mind.

Two weeks later my book was finished, and I was on a flight back to Los Angeles. I'll tell you something, though: What I found on the beach that morning—that peace of mind—I've never refound.

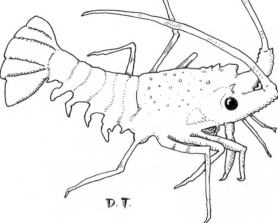

D. T.

IF FOUND, PLEASE RETURN TO...

BY FRED CHAO
with DYLAN BABB

Fred Chao writes and illustrates the comic *Johnny Hiro*. He lives in Brooklyn.

NOWADAYS, MY FREE TIME GOES TO MAKING COMICS, WHICH MEANS I DON'T GET TO WORK ON A LOT OF OTHER ART. I RARELY PAINT, FIGURE DRAW, OR WRITE SHORT STORIES ANYMORE. I ALSO DON'T GET TO SKETCH ANYMORE, WHICH I MISS MOST.

SKETCHING HAS ALWAYS APPEALED TO ME — IT FEELS LIKE ART WITHOUT CREATIVITY, LESS ABOUT ME AND MORE ABOUT TAKING IN THOSE THINGS AROUND ME AS UNFILTERED AS POSSIBLE.

SOME YEARS AGO, MUST BE SIX OR SO AT THIS POINT, I LOST A SKETCHBOOK IN LOS ANGELES.

IT COULD HAVE BEEN LEFT AT A BUS STATION OR IN A DINER. WHO KNOWS?

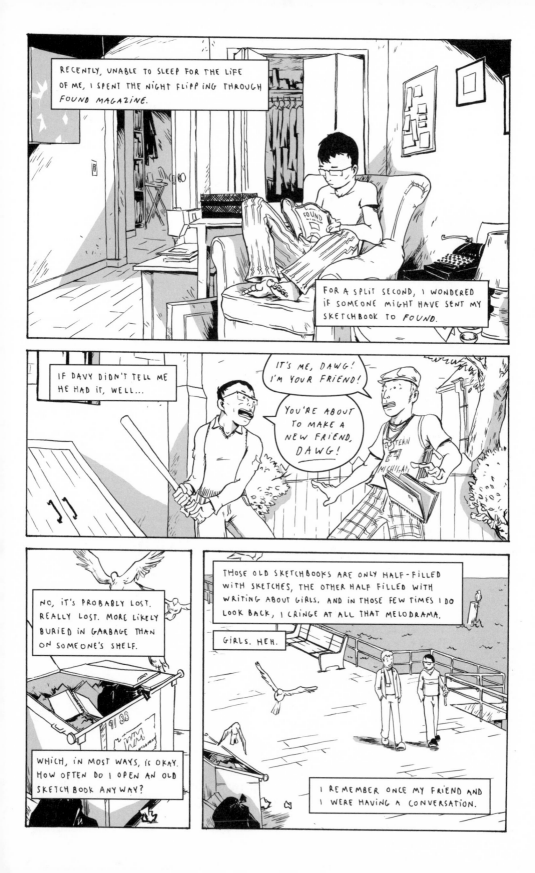

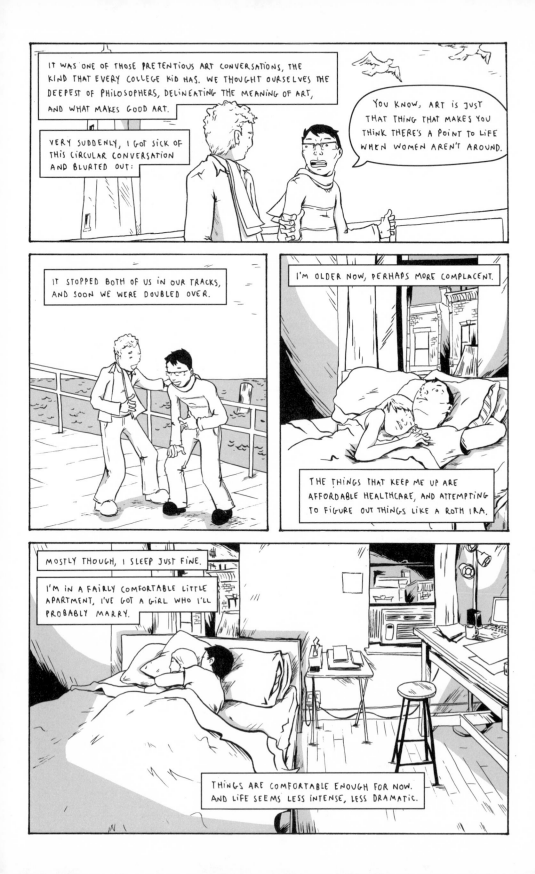

RUSSIAN HILL

Andrew Bird

Andrew Bird has released eleven albums, including *Armchair Apocrypha*. He also writes frequently for *The New York Times*.

I should have been elated—I was twenty-four years old, crossing the country on tour with my band for the first time. We reached California, and San Francisco welcomed us with its golden splendor. But there was a serious cloud hanging over my head, darkening the entire trip—I was in the middle of an agonizing breakup, the kind of situation, as everyone knows, that can make it difficult to enjoy even life's highest highs.

Our whole band was scattered across the city, sleeping on whatever couches we could beg off of friends. I woke up this particular morning to a city layered in fog, and feeling quite alone, took off on foot, headed from North Beach toward Russian Hill. There was nowhere I had to be, but a walk, it seemed, might lift away the prickly tangle of my own thoughts. After an hour, at the very top of the hill I was climbing, I saw in the distance something perched in the middle of the road. Cars kept swerving around it. From a few blocks away, I couldn't tell what it was—a sack of rice? A dead thing? I knew for certain it did not belong in the road. I quickened my pace, determined to reach whatever it was before it was destroyed by a car zooming over the crest of the hill.

As I came closer, galloping up the street and panting with the double-time effort, the shape began to materialize, until at last it formed itself into a beautiful leather Stetson hat. Not that I often donned hats like this, but it just so happened that I'd recently become enamored with a song called "The Ballad of Stack O'Lee," which tells the story of a man who murders his rival over a Stetson. I could hardly believe my luck. Things had been so awful lately, so hard and shitty and tiresome, and yet something about the hat promised a fresh start, the smile of serendipity. *This is how it's supposed to be,* I thought. *This is my hat.*

When I finally reached it, I didn't even slow my stride. I simply bent down, scooped up the hat, placed it on my head, and began the long, slow walk down the other side of the hill, lungs buoyant, ready to begin whatever came next.

THE FROG PRINCESS

Devendra Banhart

Devendra Banhart is a singer, songwriter, and musician; his most recent album is called *Smokey Rolls Down Thunder Canyon*.

At a park in San Francisco, I watched a frog sitting pensively on a large rock the size of a milk jug, looking this way and that; it was almost as though he was guarding something hidden underneath. As soon as he hopped off, I flipped the rock over and a red cockroach dashed out, the sunlight blasting it from its cave. Facedown in the moist dirt and whitened grass where the rock had been was a small photograph. I turned it over. Looking back at me was a naked Latina girl wearing only makeup and a slew of gangsta tattoos. She was standing in a bathtub in a very beautiful, sculptural-yet-comfortable yawning-cat pose, softly socking it to you in a sort of mid-nineties Janet Jackson move.

I felt instantly wowed. Was this the first time anybody had seen this picture? Or was I one of the many who were now part of her lovely exposé? Without a doubt, the picture had been hidden there—but by whom? By the girl? Had she put it under the rock to be protected by her friend the frog? Or had someone else hidden it there with the intention of retrieving it later? Had it been hidden there so no one else would find it? Perhaps it had been placed as a kind of time capsule, so that ten years in the future someone would find it and say, "Man, she sure was *fiiiiine!*" I asked myself if studying the picture was morally right or wrong. I thought, *Shit, I shouldn't be looking at this—it's intimate, personal stuff; it's like looking through someone's window*. It wasn't meant for my eyes; she'd taken the picture to send to her love.

Then, immediately, my conscience shifted its focus to her expression and locked in on the girl's true intentions, and all of my questions of morality became quickly insignificant. I realized the essence of the look in her eyes was this: "I'm communicating my beauty . . . to *you!*" *You* being whoever was gazing at the picture. It was like looking at a piece of art. I imagined that I'd encountered this radical gallery and was holding in my hands an artifact that was holy and timeless.

I thought about showing the picture to my friends and joking to them that the girl was my new girlfriend. But I also felt protective of her, possessive of her radiance. And yet it wouldn't be right, I knew, to keep her locked away in a drawer in my room. I couldn't keep the picture, and at the same time, I couldn't just throw it away. The photograph was too beautiful and passionate to be tossed.

There was, of course, another solution. After spending a few glorious days in her company, I hid the girl under another rock in another park, where I assumed a frog would once again stand guard for a couple of weeks, or maybe a couple of centuries, until the next curious wanderer found it, and the legend of the naked gangsta girl would begin again.

ZIPLOC FORTUNE COOKIE

Damian Kulash

Damian Kulash is the lead singer and guitarist for the rock band *OK Go*.

Four years ago, in L.A.'s Chinatown, I found a handwritten note on the sidewalk. It was on a six-inch lined piece of paper and tucked inside a plastic ziploc freezer bag three times its size. The note said, simply, "It is not working." It's been pinned above my desk ever since.

When I found the note, I was fighting with the writing of a song. I really hated what I was writing, and there's no place where emotional swings are more uncontrolled than in your creative work. When things are going well, you feel euphoric, but when a song is sucking, you just hate it and you hate yourself and hate everything. I was deep in one of those valleys, and here before me the news was presented in a sealed plastic bag lying on the ground: *It is not working*.

My curiosity was piqued. Why had someone made the effort to bag this thought, to protect and formalize it? From the handwriting, I guessed that the note had been written by a teenage girl. Perhaps it was an attempt to shake loose of something that wasn't working for her. If I were to articulate the same thought and seal it and toss it to the wind, might I be freed of my own bad juju? Maybe it was simply a matter of bagging it up.

On one hand, the note seemed like a comment specific to my current situation. But it also seemed like an assessment of the state of the world, like this note could have been pinned on us by aliens, as in, "The *human condition* is not working." Simply the fact that it articulated how I was feeling brought me a bit of redemption. The note helped to put my frustration in perspective, to see that my problem wasn't that big of a problem and remind me that struggle was universal. Finding it brought me out of my own head for a moment and made me feel less alone.

Del Tha Funkee Homosapien

Del Tha Funkee Homosapien is a rapper and producer from Oakland, California; his latest albums are *Deltron Event II* and *Eleventh Hour*.

Bobby. Yeah, Bobby. Let's say that's the kid's name. He's full of fear and desperation. His pops is ill, and they need money to pay the hospital bills. Bobby's got a faith in God, so he's reaching out, praying for help. In a way, he's testing God and exploring the boundaries of his own faith. He knows God's probably not going to reach down, read the note, and say, "Oh, okay, I'll give you some money." But he wants to put the thought out there, just in case. He feels God is listen-

Dear god,
my dad is very
ill, and is dying
give me money

ing. And expressing the urgency of his hopes feels important to him, even if God's not listening. The funny part of it, I think, is how he's crossed out the word *god* in god damit. At some point he must've realized that if you're writing a letter to God, you probably shouldn't say *God dammit!*

Bobby's lost in the painful questions that arise in moments like this. Why do things like this happen in life? If there's a God, why would God let his pops get so sick? I've faced these kinds of difficult situations before in my own life, and I just try to be a realist and recognize that sometimes terrible, inexplicable things happen to people. Personally, I don't believe that God is up there, pulling the strings. I'm not a religious person, but I am a spiritual person, and I've seen the value that religion can have in helping people access their own spirituality. I grew up around the church; I've just learned to tap into a spiritual power that feels separate from traditional notions of God.

The thing about a find like this is that the unfinished story lingers in your mind for weeks to come. Did Bobby's pops die? Did Bobby blame God for it and feel angry at God for ignoring his letter? When you're struck with this kind of loss, you can accept it—learn from it and build upon it—or you can refuse to accept it and lash out at the world.

But I like to believe that things went differently. I think his pops made an amazing comeback. I think somewhere Bobby is praising God for responding to his prayers.

WANTED DEAD OR ALIVE

OR ALIVE

Elizabeth Ellen

Elizabeth Ellen is the author of two chapbooks, *Before You She Was a Pit Bull* and *Sixteen Miles Outside of Phoenix*. She lives in Ann Arbor, Michigan.

My boyfriend and I were walking the dog when we came across what appeared to be the entire contents of someone's life spread out on the lawn near our apartment. Clothing, books, CDs, a couch, a suitcase, packages of ramen noodles, a hair dryer, Tampax . . . everything these people owned was right there in the grass for anyone—us—to see, go through, take. It looked as though they'd been in the middle of dinner and suddenly had to flee. There was a pot of cooked pasta that our dog kept getting into, a pair of dirty dishes.

We weren't sure what to do. We'd seen stuff like this happen in the movies, but never in real life. The voyeurs in us wanted to look. But we were worried the owners would come back and find us going through their shit. We figured they'd be pretty pissed off, given the circumstances. Then another couple came along. They didn't seem as concerned.

"This your stuff?" they asked.

"No," we said, shaking our heads.

That was all they needed to know. They gave us a half-assed shoulder shrug, then rolled up their sleeves and started digging. They looked like they'd done this before.

"Oh, look," the woman said. "*Coyote Ugly!*"

So we started digging, too. Most of the movies we'd already seen (*Big Daddy, Die Hard, Boys on the Side*) or owned (*Casino, The Deer Hunter, Planes, Trains and Automobiles*) or had no interest in (*How to Make an American Quilt*), but underneath them, at the very bottom of the box, were a handful of blank VHS tapes and we took those, hoping they were porn. (They weren't.) We grabbed a couple of books: *Seabiscuit, White Oleander,* Jenny McCarthy's *Baby Laughs,* and a CD: *Dark Side of the Moon.*

Mostly I was searching for personal stuff. Diaries, notes, mix tapes. I found a notebook and started flipping through it. It looked like a woman's handwriting. I thought I'd struck gold and found her journal. Later I realized it was less a journal and more an accounting of a catering business she was trying to start and a diet she was on, lists of foods she needed for her "business" and ones she couldn't eat on her diet. There was a lot of crossover.

At the bottom of a mildewed box I made a truly great score: a couple of generic-looking photo albums, the sort you get for five bucks at Kmart. I opened them up and began flipping through. The people inside looked immediately familiar to me—the guys with their mullets and mustaches, their Mötley Crüe/Ted Nugent/Metallica muscle shirts and acid-wash jeans, the girls drinking wine coolers out of two liters, scrunchies in their hair, oversized plastic hoops dangling from their ears, everybody smoking Marlboros and flipping the camera the bird. It was 1987 all over again and everyone, myself included, was seventeen. I'd graduated three hours away, in a small town in Ohio, but I could have sworn these were *my* classmates, the people I'd partied with, made out with, puked beside, dry-humped, gotten high with in the fall of '86 and the spring of '87, all to the tune of Bon Jovi's *Slippery When Wet*. I could practically hear "Wanted Dead or Alive" playing in the background.

Back in the privacy of our apartment I sat on the couch, the albums open on my lap, studying each picture. A majority of them seemed to have been taken in someone's basement. There was a water bed butted up against a concrete wall, water pipes running floor to ceiling, a rug thrown haphazardly on the floor. Cans of Budweiser and Coke and Miller Genuine Draft littered the coffee table and bookshelf and headboard. And everywhere teenagers sprawled: passed out on the water bed, wrestling on the floor, in a head-hold on the couch. Other photos showed them shirtless in the backseat of a Mustang; sitting on the patio step, arms draped around one another's necks; taking turns drinking directly from the keg; wearing PARTY NAKED T-shirts under a palm tree presumably somewhere in Florida; doing shots of Canadian Mist and Bacardi in a hotel room in tuxes; playing air guitar; and throwing the heavy-metal devil-horns sign; looking drunk and ecstatic and in love, on the brink of adulthood, without a care in the world, except the next day's hangover.

I felt bad about taking them, for stealing someone else's memories. But, I rationalized, I didn't have any photos to remind me of my last days of high school, no albums detailing the keg parties we'd had when someone's parents went out of town, the party I'd thrown at my grandparents' house on two consecutive weekends while they were in Florida. I'd paid dearly for it—was grounded for three months, earned an ass-beating, and, worse, my grandfather's disappointment. But it'd been worth it: I'd gotten my first fingering on the basement couch beneath photos of the plane my grandfather flew in World War II and had my first hangover in my grandparents' bed after a night of heavy sampling from their liquor cabinet. I was sure that the person who'd put together these photo albums probably had more, in a box at her parents' house, I hoped, or in an overlooked box on the lawn.

L AST YEAR WE BOUGHT A house and moved across town. Somewhere along the way the blank tapes and notebook and Jenny McCarthy book got thrown out. But I still have the photo albums. I don't ever plan on throwing them away. I keep them on a shelf in my office. I like having them there to take down and look at from time to time, to remind me of what I've almost forgotten.

On the inside of one of the albums it reads: SENIORS, 87–88, HURON HIGH SCHOOL. The people in these photos, men and women my age now, graduated from a school down the street from where we live. We drive by it on a near-daily basis. Most of them probably still live in town. We likely cross paths with them and never even know it: at Whole Foods or my kid's school or the local sports bar. Our kids might be friends, in the same class, ride the same bus; they might one day graduate together, get high together, lose their virginity together, party naked together. If they do, I hope they take lots of pictures, pictures to fill albums or discard on wet lawns, pictures for themselves or someone else to find in years to come.

Photo found by Elizabeth Ellen,
Ann Arbor, MI

AL-ZAWAHIRI'S LETTER

Michael Yon

Michael Yon is the author of the book *Moment of Truth in Iraq* and continues to blog from Iraqi towns and battlefields.

In 2005, I was living in Mosul, in northern Iraq. There in the city, a letter was found during a raid, discovered on the hard drive of a confiscated computer. I was lucky enough to be one of the only journalists to see the letter, as it was classified top secret as soon as it was found.

The letter was written by Ayman al-Zawahiri, who, at the time, was second in command for Al-Qaeda, and addressed to Abu Musab al-Zarqawi. Over thirteen pages, he argued with passion and eloquence against the "slaughtering" (cutting throats) of hostages. This kind of act had become well-known around the world, and al-Zawahiri complained that it was making them look bad. He said that most Muslims have hearts, and that they were losing supporters because of these horrific and public killings. He warned al-Zarqawi to stop listening to the faithful supporters who were urging him to continue to authorize the slaughters, and begged him to understand that the average Muslim opposed them. I've witnessed the brutality and savagery of the terrorist clans, and al-Zawahiri's call for restraint took me by surprise.

However, it was his solution to this ongoing problem that made this find so truly stunning and gave me such a powerful understanding of his mind's inner workings. After eleven pages, pleading with al-Zarqawi to stop the grisly killings, al-Zawahiri said, essentially, "Look, quit cutting off the hostages' heads in public; quit making a big scene out of it. Instead, just shoot them in the head and dump them in the desert. It's not the savagery that's important, it's not the spectacle, it's just the killing that counts." I'd been mistaken—he didn't want the murdering to stop, he just didn't want to risk Al-Qaeda's popularity slipping among moderate Muslims.

I've seen a lot happen over here, but that chilling letter has always stuck with me.

MONOPLY MONOPLY & private Business
  private
Full-Time Leaders Emergent Leaders
University Local - training group
Trg - center
convent EMPYL
Seminary
many of recieve training when they are
young. they are orientated
toward life issues and one easily - dis
couraged by theory which seems unrelated to life
What we means by team different
things.
the different
of minist

cation Ordering
Southern Aerash

We ma
For they
We must realize
(to select and tr
(to develop Fully Re

the congregation of St. Simon
dependences - First Reading is taken
From prophets isiah isiah 13-25-28 -
na ye raan La guop a dummuom Ku akuec
adummuom bital araan path, Ku
Bai, ke yen abi piinc,
ulo to pilipiiians -
buon bi thou

117½ maloes -
     4½   14
        22½   28
Se   23 39   4
     6 Y 6 5 60
54 6)216 29 356   24
29 -18   wood work
84   58   2 sack 24 price
     58   350
  3 sacks 2 maloes

Sothern y y y
Sothern v you you you you you you
  going. goes goes.
To must prepare
For key responsibilities
must which which which which which
Whoping select when when when when
ought to develop Fully Responsible
Do not count your eggs before hatch
Borrow meat of cow was been killed, to bor
out by Sorghum - The advantages of central
d training are- The Trainess can more easily be tempt
to adopt a superiority Adultry
committee of the Red cows cross-
  Hear 2000 thousand
  crocs- cow dung

November 199c
seph is one of a large
each of his
His mother

EGGS BEFORE THEY HATCH

Dave Eggers

**Dave Eggers is the author of the memoir *A Heartbreaking Work of
Staggering Genius* and the novels *You Shall Know Our Velocity*
and *What Is the What*.**

I t's weird, because I consider myself a pack rat—I keep just about every
piece of paper with any vague significance—and at the same time, I also
try to be open to finding things like those that appear in *FOUND*. But in all the
years I've been reading *FOUND*, no matter how hard I've tried, I've never found
anything odd or funny enough to appear in the magazine. I've actually only
picked up a handful of stray papers in all that time, and most of them have
been in southern Sudan. I've collected a bunch of interesting papers there, all
but one of them fished out of garbage cans and about to be incinerated.

The piece of paper shown here I found in 2003, in Marial Bai, the remote
hometown of my friend Valentino Deng—about whom I wrote *What Is the
What*. I found this piece of paper before the peace agreement was signed, and
the war between the Sudanese government and the rebel army was still tech-
nically being fought. Schools weren't in session in any real sense, and in any
case, this was a rural area, where there were few books, pencils and pens, or
paper. When Valentino and I were walking around one day, I found this piece
of paper in a field, within ten yards of a huge ostrich. I picked up the piece of

paper, tried to find a name on it so I could return it, but failing at that, I kept it in my journal.

It's a fascinating piece of paper, signifying a lot of things. First of all, because paper was so scarce at that time in that part of Sudan—it continues to be scarce everywhere—whoever wrote on this page was conserving space as much as possible. The writer seems to be a student, maybe of high school age, and he or she was copying down certain words and phrases. It's evident that the instructor was jumping around a bit, or else the student used this single sheet of paper for all sorts of different classes. You see the words "cow dung" near "the advantages of centralized training" and those words near "adultery" and the expression "do not count your eggs before hatch." There's math being done here, verb conjugations, Bible studies, and also this revelation: "They are orientated towards life issues and one easily discouraged by theory which seems unrelated to life."

I've shown both sides of the page, hoping to demonstrate how determined this student was to learn, despite the limited resources available. Everywhere we went on that trip, we saw students using pre-used paper for their writing, using newsprint (or actually using newspaper and writing over the print). I hope it's implicit how well used any educational materials are in remote areas like Marial Bai, where books and paper (not to mention schools, teachers, chairs, etc.) are too scarce.

Fortunately, conditions in southern Sudan have improved a lot since 2003. The peace agreement was signed in 2005, and there is new development all over the region, with hundreds of thousands of refugees returning to their homes. When Valentino and I returned to Marial Bai in 2007, the schools were in session and about a thousand kids were attending primary school in the town. The facilities were ailing, the teachers wanted more assistance and training, and the books and paper and materials were still far too scarce.

After that trip, we formed the Valentino Achak Deng Foundation, with Valentino as executive director. He's spending most of 2008 in Marial Bai—he's there as I'm writing—building a secondary school, a dorm, a library, and a community center, and will be bringing as many books, workbooks, and learning materials as he can transport from Uganda and Kenya (he bought two trucks for the purpose). Things are moving in the right direction.

REQUIEM FOR A PAPER BAG

Drew Daniel

Drew Daniel is a professor of English at Johns Hopkins University. His band, Matmos, just released their seventh album, *Supreme Balloon*.

My friend Lecie found it at the MacArthur BART station in Oakland and promptly gave it to me. It was a brown paper bag, folded into thirds and written upon, with certain key phrases emphatically underlined, and a tidily specific sum inscribed sideways in the margins ($4.32). Strokes of black ballpoint pen had transformed the bag into what at first looked like a to-do list, but once you read it you weren't so sure. At once a poem, diary entry, incomplete testimonial, and a token of someone's fraught existence, the transcript runs as follows:

Gremmy

CRACK COCAIN LOSHIT

Shitting in newspapers and on

Shoe boxes

Throwing food out the window

Smoking Low cigarettes

Taking Lemons off the trees

Taking Loquarts off trees

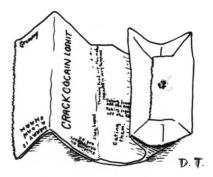

Eating them. Takeing

Putting Pee In the Ground

Garbage bins back here

LARRY IS A LOAN SHARK

Vocational Rehabilitation

Street Cleaning

Sweep Cleaning

Garbage Trucks (3) III

Mop the toilet bowl

Putting bleech on the floor

Mopping It

[address on San Pablo Avenue]

Insurance Man

Who or what was "Gremmy"? Was it someone's name? Was it a phoneti-cization of hurried speech: "Grab my crack cocaine" becoming "Gremmy crack cocain" in the sneeze and flush of a high, or in the rush of writing? Who is speaking here? How do they live? What are "Low" cigarettes? Butts found on the street? An off-brand? Gremmy crack corn and I don't care. These are mysteries. What I do know is that whoever wrote this has their own way with language. Though the author can't quite spell rehabilitation, they get close, and switch back pretty breezily between Arabic and Roman numerals. The micro-Beckett play of demi-homeless urban misery is there in sharp focus: loan sharks, mopping toilet stalls, nowhere to shit but the street. But its pain is belied by the author's effortless recall of tart, summery details; the loquats and lemons, and the moments of behavior that go beyond scarcity and into unexpected abundance and abandon. Putting pee in the ground is all very well, but throwing food out the window?

T

HE BAG BECAME A KIND of flag for me at an important point of change in my life. I had just moved in with my boyfriend Martin and we started a band of sorts. At the time we were in the first bloom of our love affair with each other and with musique concrète, the French technique of constructing musical forms by manipulating found sounds sourced from everyday life rather than from traditional musical instruments. Trying to work with whatever we had ready in-hand in our Tenderloin tenement apartment rather than the "infinite possibilities" of synthesis and software, we sampled the sounds of domestic junk and quotidian objects (bowls of water, our hair, random thrift-store finds). We would scavenge by day for raw materials and then stay up till dawn chopping and reassembling the results into primitive songs. After some false starts and some heartfelt rejection letters from various corners, we stubbornly decided to take the plunge and put out our own music, pressing our first compact disc ourselves in an edition of one thousand (to us at the time an ominously large and presumptuous number, though it was the manufacturer's minimum). We called our vanity label Vague Terrain, in part because that was the name of the French comic book publisher that had first put out the original graphic novel of *Barbarella*, but also because it meant a junkyard, an urban landscape of unwanted scrap and crap. A *terrain vague* was precisely the sort of place in which one might expect to find something like the mysterious paper bag. In our attempt to transpose our approach to audio into a visual form, this bag functioned as found liner notes: physical evidence that was more arresting than anything we could write or invent ourselves. We scanned and included the image of the bag inside our booklet, thus disseminating our treasured find to the random strangers who might somehow stumble onto our own efforts before our CD made its way to the landfill, in turn. We aspired to have each of our mechanically reproduced copies of the paper bag saturated with its own material specificity, so we decided to create by hand a different collage inside the CD tray of every copy. The result of this rash vow was hours upon hours of collage parties around the kitchen table, as housemates and gullible friends mulched through stacks of *National Geographics*, tossing nicotine patches, hair, and tabs of LSD into the mix for good measure, gluing and slicing abject little scenes into place. We were almost disappointed when distributor orders trickled from a few to thirty to three hundred at a time and we had to repress the album, because the en-masse-collage turnover rate became pretty punishing. All along I felt as if I was playing catch-up with the weird charisma of the creator of the mysterious bag. My bird-headed women and scissored waterfalls were dutifully Max Ernst earnest and my abstract slivers of shapes were suitably Schwitters-y but never quite matched the decisive oomph of Gremmy CRACK COCAIN LOSHIT.

I**T'S** **BEEN** **ALMOST** **THIRTEEN** **YEARS** since Lecie found that paper bag, and inevitably, some things have changed. The bag means something different to me now. Its text has stayed the same, but its raw sadness has clarified considerably. The other night a formerly close friend of ours from San Francisco, whom I'll call "Bob," called us up. Bob had always been a drug-gobbling fiend over the weekends, and I'd had my share of long strange trips with him during my undergrad years, spelunking into hallucinogenic wormholes (once he turned into a chicken before my goggling eyes) before coming back up to reality for fresh air. We'd made music together, traveled in Europe together, gone record shopping together, and partied a great deal. Things had somehow slid wildly out of control since he hooked up with his new boyfriend. Weeping and desperately ashamed, Bob told me that he was now in rehab for a three-headed monster of addictions: alcohol, methadone, and crack. He'd had to move out of his apartment in the Tenderloin and crash at a clean-and-sober friend's place because he couldn't trust himself to come home from work with pay in hand and walk past his dealers on the corner. He knew that he'd just fuck up and get high. In one binge, he and his boyfriend had spent $800 on crack in a single weekend. He'd nearly lost everything, and he couldn't imagine how he was going to crawl out of the wreckage. I tried to think of supportive and reassuring things to say, and I said them and meant them.

It wasn't until I put down the phone that it hit me. Looking back at my own years of living in the Tenderloin and then Oakland and then the Mission, I realized that I had been in it but not of it, floating serenely across the poverty and predation around me, somehow hip to it and savvy enough to watch my back (mostly—I got robbed at gunpoint once and randomly punched in the head once), but not really bothered by it and never really marked by any of it. All that time I had been an onlooker. The thought that one of my own friends would turn into a crackhead was, somehow, unthinkable, simply outside the parameters of my white-college-kid, middle-class-liberal default settings. I think now about the way that I prized that paper bag then. Was there something spurious and touristy about it? Was I just slumming, trying to extract some "primitive" heat from a found fetish, taking a cheap holiday in other people's misery? Would I have cared as much about the bag if it hadn't arrived garishly emblazoned with the words "CRACK COCAIN" across the top? It stood in for a poor urban underclass that everyone's already exhausted thinking about—"the poor ye have always with ye"—the, by definition, not-me. At some level, wasn't the bag permitting me a temporary high of my own? Hadn't it given me the cozy, superior feeling of pressing myself up against the glass barrier of the socioeconomic zoo to leer at an exotic life-form, a weird loser, a total reject that shits in shoe boxes, somebody that I would probably never talk to but could feel endlessly curious about once they were safely out of sight? I don't know the answers to these questions about the person who wrote on this grocery bag, and I may never discover the backstory to Lecie's find. I hope its author has a better life now—one that wouldn't turn my hope that they are still alive into a backhanded curse. When I first encountered it, the paper bag felt like a fitting emblem for my own desire to be receptive to what was around me; to listen carefully, save what I could, share what I'd found. But with time it gets harder and harder to define exactly what that paper bag was saying.

MY FOUND LIFE

Michael Musto

Michael Musto is a columnist for the *Village Voice* and a pop culture commentator on MSNBC.

G lancing around my one-bedroom Manhattan apartment, friends have always thrilled to the kitschy clutter and wondered just how much it all cost. "Nothing," I've always replied, nonchalantly. While other people unearth a fifty-dollar ashtray at a flea market and call it a real find, I *literally* come up with real finds—things I've run into through years of biking around the item-strewn streets of New York. It's an amazingly reasonable way to shop. As someone who's been addicted to the comp lifestyle since my aunt—the nun—got us in to see *The Sound of Music* for free, it also really appeals to my whorish side to nab some decor for nothing. Fueling this impulse, New York, for all its Disney-esque sheen these days, is still studded with saucy street garbage and luscious litter. People abandon incredible things for all sorts of reasons—or maybe they just accidentally drop them—and as the Angelina Jolie of discarded objects, I'll gladly adopt them and give them a home.

One of my favorite found artworks is a painting of a child who looks sort of like a young Tuesday Weld, with California-blonde hair and vivid, almost almondy eyes that fix right on you. This girl isn't precious or Keane-like, she's direct, not begging for any sympathy whatsoever. Ever since finding her on a

Murray Hill sidewalk ten years ago, I've wondered who this confident waif is and whether she has a backstory. But that's the joy of found art—you have no idea what (or whom) you're hanging on your wall.

My other beloved found piece is easier to demystify. It's a big Joe Camel head on a base that plugs in and lights up to say all sorts of promotional things about Camel cigarettes. Someone from a store had obviously tossed this to the wind, probably around the time when people stopped smoking. Lugging the thing home, I developed biceps, and, as it turns out, some character. I recently ended up giving Joe to a friend who needed some cash, so if *you* want to find my found object, kindly look on eBay.

D. T.

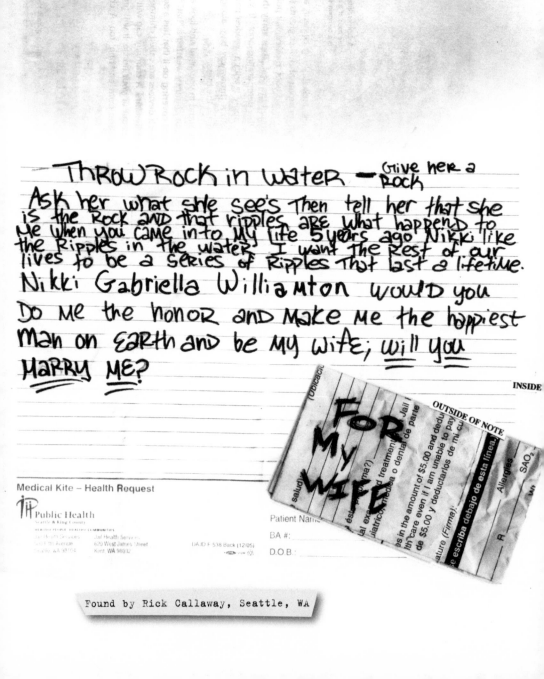

THROW ROCK in WATER — Give her a Rock
Ask her what she see's Then tell her that she
is the Rock and that ripples are what happenD to
Me when you came into My life 5 years ago Nikki like
the Ripples in the water I want The Rest of our
lives to be a series of ripples That last a lifetime.
Nikki Gabriella Williamton would you
Do Me the honor and Make Me the happiest
Man on EaRth and be My wife; will you
MARRY ME?

INSIDE

FOR My WIFE

OUTSIDE OF NOTE

Medical Kite – Health Request

Public Health
Seattle & King County

HEALTHY PEOPLE HEALTHY COMMUNITIES
Jail Health Services   Jail Health Services
300 9th Avenue   620 West James Street   DAJD F 538 Back (12/05)
Seattle, WA 98104   Kent, WA 98032

Patient Name

BA #:

D.O.B.:

THE BLONDE

Tom Robbins

Tom Robbins is the author of eight novels, including *Even Cowgirls Get the Blues* and *Still Life with Woodpecker*; his latest book is *B Is for Beer*.

This is one of my favorite finds—I love the careful planning that this man has put into his marriage proposal. Oddly, it makes me recall a marriage proposal I once received, one that seemed to have had no planning at all. I'll tell you the story.

Back in the day, I used to do these poetry readings at a beatnik coffeehouse in Richmond, Virginia. The café was in the bohemian district of Richmond, nestled right next to the School of Art. A small improvisational jazz trio played behind me as I read my poems, many of which were political, like a lot of beat poetry; I was especially critical of Southern gentility.

The audience each night was your typical array of black-clad youth with berets and pipes, all except for one strikingly beautiful blonde woman. She was clearly from the west end of Richmond, the affluent part of the city. Though I was attracted to her, she also brought out a certain hostility in me. She clearly wasn't a beatnik, nor did she live close by, so I assumed she must be slumming. My resentment of her came to a head one October night when I was in the middle of one of my poems about the Richmond aristocracy and she got up and stormed out of the bar. I figured that would be the last I'd see of her.

A couple of weeks later, I had to make a trip downtown—I was fighting a realty company about the apartment I was living in and things weren't going my way. I left their office extremely frustrated and red-faced. It was a hot day, so I ducked into the nearest drinking establishment and ordered a cold beer to ease both my temperature and my temperament.

I was sitting at the bar, still seething, when the beautiful blonde stranger came in. I turned around on my barstool, and before I could stop myself, I lit into her for walking out of the café that day while I was reading my poetry. I told her that I loved Richmond but stood by my criticisms, and who the hell was she to simply walk out? I went on and on and on, pouring out my whole day's frustrations on her. She didn't say a word. She just stood there in that bar, mouth agape. Eventually, I ran out of steam. She stood there a moment longer, blinked once, and said simply, "Will you marry me?"

At the time, I was romantically involved with a Jewish girl. Her parents liked me well enough, but when they found out we were really serious about each other, they forbade me from seeing her anymore; they wanted her to marry a Jewish guy. She kept a Jewish boyfriend as a cover so that we could steal visits here and there, but the whole situation was beginning to wear on me. So when I accepted the marriage proposal from this beautiful blonde woman, whom I'd never spoken to before that night, I suppose I was trying to blow myself out of that impasse and be done with that impossible relationship.

The blonde and I finished our drinks and then went back to my house and made love in the backyard, after which her proposal seemed all the more attractive. The next day, we drove to the home of a minister we knew of in North Carolina and were married there on the spot. We'd only told a few people that we were going to get married and they were all horrified. I didn't care. There was something incredibly titillating about marrying someone I didn't know. Marriage is such an intimate proposition. To suddenly achieve that kind of intimacy with someone—not through a one-night stand, but an ostensible commitment—well, there was something pretty erotic about it.

Sometimes it's necessary to grab that metaphorical dynamite and blow your life to pieces. I never harbored any delusions that this marriage would work, but I still think it was absolutely the best decision I could have made at that time. It was like getting up in the middle of the night, packing up all of my belongings, driving to some unknown destination, and calling it home. The blonde was my second wife, and I was married to her for three years.

I've never been the asker, but I've had marriage proposed to me a few times since, and I've always accepted. I have a hard time saying no.

Sheri, here is a song written by Stryper, &
want you to read it & understand what it
means to me.
I wish I had wrote it, because it tells
exactly how I feel about you.

I've searched for a true love
for such a long long time,
now my search has ended,

THE SHERI MILLER STORY

Al Burian

Al Burian makes a 'zine called *Burn Collector* and plays in the bands Milemarker and Challenger. He is also the author of the book *Things Are Meaning Less*.

1.

Back in the mythological mid-nineties, when our earth still seemed like it might have a future, I was engaged in the standard idealistic pursuits of my generation: living in a punk house, starving myself on a steady diet of dumpstered bagels, setting up shows in the living room, and sneaking out the back when the landlord would come banging on the front door. This happened pretty often. We were on rent strike, and the realty office was located right across the street.

Mr. Tate, the landlord, was a notorious character around town. He was reputed to be involved in all manner of shady and illegal activities, not the least ominous of which was burning down his own property in order to collect on the insurance. We were in over our heads. Tate was an intimidating guy, huge and menacing, with resonant, thundering fists. He'd beat on the door, standing outside with his cronies, threatening us with eviction and devastating bodily harm in a rich, sonorous baritone. We'd cower, shaking and giddy with fear.

The house itself was a dilapidated shack and had been sitting unoccupied for quite some time before our arrival. The first night we moved in, we discovered that this vacancy wasn't exactly vacant: There were ragged piles of clothes, some crack-smoking paraphernalia, and the back door had been pried open—telltale signs that someone was squatting on the premises. We left the items on the back porch with an apologetic note: "Hi. We've moved in here now, we are sorry if we're displacing you," signed with hearts and smiley faces. The next morning we discovered that the items had been retrieved and our letter had been responded to, a parting gift left to us on the doorstep: In a shoe box was a steamy pile of human shit.

2.

OUR MATERIAL CONDITIONS SEEMED TO speak against victory. The plumbing was shot, the stove didn't work, and there was obvious major structural damage to the building. Also, there was a rat, skittering among our sleeping bags in the night. It took a lot of concentration to maintain our utopian vision.

But we were determined. Springing into action, we scoured the streets at night, looking through the trash for furniture, building supplies, food, art, and inspiration, locating these things in the waking-world's garbage. We didn't believe that you ever had to buy anything; it seemed that we could fulfill our every need simply by looking. In a college town, with its constant turnover of transient student population and an affluent class of professorial types, this turned out to be an exceedingly correct assumption. It was all there for the taking. One could build an entire existence from the scraps of other people's lives, the things that they could find no use for. There seemed no end to the things people would let go of.

It was a case of idealism run amok, taken to irrational extremes. By the time we reneged on paying the rent, we'd grown cultish and loopy. Property was theft, we told anyone who would listen, and you could no more own this corner of Mitchell Lane than you could the air or the sun. Our ideology was outrageous, but the raw audacity of our actions gave them a compelling adrenaline edge. We were living free, going up against the Man, our house shows and art projects facing down his brutal, thuggish reality. We seemed to be winning, for the moment. It seemed crazily possible that we might just get away with it.

3

ONE DAY, EXPLORING A SHED in the backyard, my roommate found a treasure trove. Boxed up and left behind in the shed was a collection of letters, photographs, high school yearbooks, and other ephemera—a time capsule, the life of another person entombed in cardboard. Perusing these things led us to decipher that they belonged to a woman named Sheri Miller. She'd apparently occupied the shitbox some years before us and seemingly left in a hurry, if leaving behind such a cache of personal sentimental items was any indication. Or had she left them behind intentionally? It seemed hard to imagine. Who would want to rid themselves of these items, the delicate ballpoint penmanship of high school sweethearts, notes passed illicitly back and forth in math class?

Sheri Miller, whose life seemed so ordinary and un-insane. I was fascinated by the documentation, at the glimpse into a past that had deposited her, somehow, in this same strange circumstance, living in this horrible little house. The letters and pictures told an elaborate story, sketched the shores of an epic romance. There was so much possibility. How had she ended up living in the squalid shack across from Tate Realty? What was the missing piece of the story that had gotten her here?

4

I PONDERED HER FATE, KNOWING THAT my considerations were futile. This was in an age before people were Google-able. The questions were unanswerable. There was no way I'd find Sheri.

These days anyone can be found instantly, with no effort. Type in the name and click: Born in North Carolina, she now lives in Vermont. When she is not tap-dancing, she is reciting haiku into a handheld tape recorder. Married with two children, she enjoys sailing and music. Residing in the suburbs outside of Washington, D.C., Sheri Miller works for the American Pharmacists Association. Or, she is a helicopter pilot working at a hospital in Massachusetts. She might also be a drug counselor at a Christian academy in Myrtle Beach, South Carolina. Sheri has an irresistible smile that brightens any room she's in. She thanks God that things worked out exactly the way they did, and claims that she does not regret the hard times, as they were part of what made her who she is today. There is senior account representative Sheri Miller, just as there is lesbian health care activist Sheri Miller. Or she may be an ordained minister of the gnostic faith, albeit one whose flashy, special-effects-intensive website would seem to belie the very tenets of her faith.

And so on and so forth. There are hundreds, maybe thousands, of versions of Sheri out there, all living wildly different lives. It is as if she left her one self behind in that cardboard box to splinter into a hundred incarnations, as if she has become a universe unto herself. I am lost in that universe, in her ethereal sphere, the vortex of Sheri.

So the question appears to be unanswerable after all. I know the intimate details of her past, and yet it has all added up to no future—or rather, there is a future, but I cannot decipher what it is. I have stayed on course, remained consistent, followed a straight line to a terminus point. Sheri, meanwhile, has exploded in all directions.

5.

ONE NIGHT, THERE WAS A knock at the door. I was startled from my reading of her letters, snapped awkwardly back into reality, and suddenly I knew: I knew that knock. It was Sheri, back to collect her yearbooks, her love notes, here to reclaim her life. I held my breath, anticipating our meeting, finally, face to face.

When I opened the door, I was surprised to find Mr. Tate standing there.

"This building is not up to code," he explained calmly, as if it had just suddenly come to his attention. "There are problems with the wiring. You'd better move out right away. I get a feeling the place could burn down any day now." The message delivered, he turned and walked back across the street to his office.

We got the hint and moved out the next day. Sure enough, Fort Shitbox burned to the ground within the week, taking the collected memories of Sheri Miller with it.

MITCHELL LANE LOOKS DIFFERENT NOW: all the hopes and ideals of youth, buried under a parking garage attached to a newly built condominium complex. Tate sold the property to developers a few years ago; that's how things go. You get used to it. You gain nothing by focusing on loss, but it is also undeniable that we lose more than we find. We are clinging to the scraps, trying to forge a future from them, but the bulldozers are closing in all around us.

A few blocks away from where I used to live, there is a new house that's filled with new kids doing exciting things. I am living in a shed behind this house. People think I've fallen on hard times, but actually my times have remained about the same. Things aren't so bad in the shed; the price is right and I have all the bagels I can eat. My meager belongings are boxed up in the corner, and were I to mysteriously disappear one day, future generations could unearth me, archaeologically, sifting through the debris in search of who I was.

In the evenings, I'll go into the house and join the punks for a meal. There is a calming continuity to their existence. The kitchen cupboards are overflowing with free food, while in the living room, band practices, political protests, and play rehearsals are being planned. In the hall, a stack of books salvaged from the oblivion of the PTA garbage waits in limbo for a new life, to be sent in the mail to a prisoner or given away to a friend. There is fiery, zealous conversation about gentrification, reclaiming space, and autonomous zones.

The material world yields. It gives itself away. All you have to do is stay open to it. Reach out your hand and feel it brush up against everything that's possible.

Jeans

Asian women have petite stature, but their half-length easy to get weight as a result of lacking of sports and sitting in the office for a long time. Day by day, helplessly, the thigh meets the buttocks in the shape of pear or apple. Especially, when putting on jeans, the buttock is apparent. So if the design can figure out slim waist and pretty legs, it is just what

JEANS

Rachel DeWoskin

Rachel DeWoskin is the author of the memoir _Foreign Babes in Beijing_.

On a flight from Beijing to Shanghai, I found this uniquely worded scrap of paper wadded up in the back pocket of an airplane seat. For some reason, perhaps the compelling nature of its content, another flier had stuffed it in the pocket next to the barf bag and shiny emergency-instruction pamphlet. As the kind of person who might also have mined this piece, I sat pondering both who was saving it for later and how I (or anyone trapped on a plane) could hope to avoid the disastrous fate described so brilliantly in the text: "Day by day, helplessly, the thigh meets the buttocks in the shape of pear or apple." As I studied the scrap, the flight attendants were industriously serving lunch boxes containing six types of bread, a slab of unidentifiable meat, and a bag of dried fish so pungent that when I opened it I thought I might go blind. After surveying the contents of the snack, I closed the box and turned my attention back to the scrap of paper. The scrap suddenly seemed to me—perhaps in the delirium of hunger—to offer more than your usual fashion fare, although it had that, too. Of course there's the mystery of where the plot leads: "So if the design can figure out slim waist and pretty legs, it is just what"—Just what _what_?

Just what every especially apparent buttock needs? Just what I need? Just what Air China recommends post-carbohydrate-and-cuttlefish food coma?

More than the suspense of a shredded thought on the fate of easy-to-get-weight frames, though, the beloved scrap had the specificity of language written without access to cliché, the most delightful kind of English. My favorite poems and essays almost always come from students for whom English is not native; the best one ever was written by an eleven-year-old Taiwanese boy named Martin. The assignment was simply to write a poem that rhymed (we read Shel Silverstein for inspiration). Martin wrote a poem about his friend in the class and called the masterpiece "The Stupid Jeff." It went like this: "The stupid Jeff are having cough / He cutting medicine into half. / The stupid Jeff are playing golf / He hitting ball up onto roof. / The stupid Jeff are playing in fall. / He eat the leaf and then he barf."

Martin stood before me, Jeff, and the other two ESL students in our class and recited that poem fifteen years ago, and I still remember it with absolute precision and wild hilarity. There's a shared element between the kind of poetry written in somewhat-known languages and the kind found in lost papers. Each exists in the in-between, somewhere after the sender sends it and before the receiver gets it, never reaching the exact destination for which it was designed. Neither kind of writing ends up sending precisely the message it means to, but instead delivers both more and less. Like all found treasures, words that are lost and found in translation, like those found floating through the world, create a conversation and a language all their own.

WHAT GOES UP MUST COME DOWN

Mohsin Hamid

Mohsin Hamid is an author who grew up in Lahore, Pakistan. His most recent book is *The Reluctant Fundamentalist*.

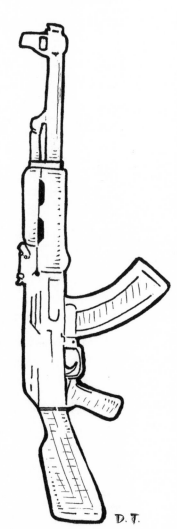

Back in 1988, I was living in Pakistan. It was my senior year of high school, and my dad had just gotten a job in the Philippines, so I was at home in Lahore with only my mom and little sister. One day my mom, really upset, woke me up. She said, "What were you doing last night?"

I could think of a number of plausible things for her to be upset about that were related to what I had been doing the night before while I was out at a party with the family car, but I had no idea how she could have been aware of any of those things. So I responded, "Nothing." Then she asked me to follow her downstairs. I went down and she took me out to the car—at the time we had an old copper-colored 1981 Toyota Corolla. The man who worked as our night guard, Ali Nawaz, was standing in front of the

D. T.

car, and as I looked closer, I saw an indentation buried in the hood of the Corolla, right up at the front toward the grille. I moved closer, somewhat baffled. Ali Nawaz was stooped over this puncture in the hood trying to get a grip on something in the hole, and finally he managed to wriggle it out. At this point, I still had no idea what he and my mother were so alarmed by, but as I reached Ali Nawaz, I saw that what he'd found in the hood of the car and was now holding in his hand was a bullet. Ali held it up high and said one word: "Kalashnikov."

Now, during the 1980s, when the Soviet-Afghanistan War was building, all sorts of weaponry began flooding into Pakistan. "Kalashnikov," or the AK-47 assault rifle, became a household word. There was also an influx of heroin because much of the war was financed using drug money. Lahore and many other big cities found themselves awash in guns and drugs.

Still, I had no idea where this bullet could possibly have come from. I didn't have a Kalashnikov, and I doubted that any of my friends had one, and even if they did, I couldn't imagine how a bullet from one had lodged itself in the hood of the car. Ali Nawaz dropped the thing into my palm. My mother had a wild, upset look, so I said, "Mom, I have no idea where this bullet came from." She said, "Look, our car has been parked inside the gate all night; the gate was locked. *You* took it out and *you* brought it home!"

Mystified, I began a kind of Lieutenant Columbo investigation right there in front of my mom and Ali Nawaz. I didn't know much about ballistics, but I figured that if somebody had shot a Kalashnikov point-blank at the hood of an '81 Corolla, the bullet would go straight through to the engine block. *What the hell could have happened?* It was a true riddle. Then in a flash it came to me: Somebody had fired a Kalashnikov straight up into the air and the bullet had come down exactly where my car happened to be parked. Meanwhile, I was inside at the party, unaware. What goes up must come down.

I began pleading my case to my mom while Ali Nawaz looked on. I pointed out the bullet's angle of entry to her, which was almost precisely vertical. I explained that either somebody had run up to the car and pointed the rifle's barrel straight down onto the hood, or that the bullet was the result of gravity, paired with an irresponsible act of celebration. When people had weddings or various celebratory occasions, often someone would fire Kalashnikov bullets into the air as if they were fireworks. I begged my mom to believe me, that I had not been in a gunfight and that this was simply what happened when one of these casually fired bullets came down.

She squinted at me, trying my explanation on for size. She seemed to believe that I hadn't gotten myself involved with any kind of gang warfare; but at the same time, she feared this kind of thing, and the story I was offering felt a bit too simple and compact to her. Guns had become common, and, as in any city with too many guns in people's hands, every so often kids would get into fights and someone would get shot. There we stood, the three of us in the driveway, caught in a strange web of mystery and concern: the night guard Ali Nawaz, my mom, and me, blinking in the morning light and staring at this little bullet. Oddly, the fact that my mom believed I might have been shot at made me feel older, as though I was capable of battle. By a fluke, I'd changed from a boy into a man.

I took the bullet and put it into the zipper pocket in my wallet. I called it my lucky bullet, and I held on to it throughout my last year of high school. Wherever I went, it went. I could always feel its bulge inside the wallet. After high school was over, I went to America for college. The first day in the dorm, I showed off the bullet to my new roommate. "This is what happens in Pakistan," I told him. "Bullets appear in the hood of your car." Instantly, I earned a reputation as some kind of war veteran, simply because of this benign bullet. I played it up, enjoying the mystique, though I knew I hadn't done anything to earn my lucky bullet. Still, it was true; I had this bent-out-of-shape Kalashnikov bullet in my wallet that used to be in the hood of my car. It changed the way I thought of myself and the way that other people thought of me—I was a guy-whose-car-was-hit-by-a-Kalashnikov-bullet-one-night kind of guy.

A couple of years later, on a trip home to Pakistan during the holidays, it occurred to me that I shouldn't try to fly with a bullet in my wallet, so I took the bullet out of the zipper pocket and put it into one of my duffel bags. I checked my bags on the flight, and when I got to Pakistan I couldn't find the bullet. I was upset that I'd lost it, and found it hard to explain to everyone why

I was so upset. Just as unexpectedly as the bullet had appeared, it had also disappeared.

But the bullet reappeared a couple of years later, in a different kind of way. In the final semester of my senior year of college, I applied to be in a creative writing class taught by Toni Morrison, and was thrilled to find out that I'd been accepted. It was a long-form fiction workshop in which you could try your hand at writing the first draft of a novel. I began what turned out to be my first novel, *Moth Smoke*. I wrote an entire first draft—a couple hundred pages in the three months that I had—and these pages were the basis of the novel that eventually got published several years later.

In *Moth Smoke*, the main character's mother has just died as the novel begins. She dies while sleeping on the roof. Families often sleep on the roofs in Pakistan because when it gets really hot, it's cooler on the rooftop with the breeze blowing. In the book, the family is sleeping up on the roof, and a random Kalashnikov bullet fired in celebration comes down and hits the main character's mother and kills her, though no one notices at first. When he wakes up in the morning, his mom is dead.

In many ways, that bullet becomes an important metaphor in the novel: for instance, people in Pakistan acting without being aware of the consequences of their actions. The Pakistan of my childhood was a place of near-misses, a dictatorship—drugs and weapons were pouring in and we had little voice in how our country was being run. This was all a big part of what I was trying to explore with *Moth Smoke*, so it made sense that this bullet would also drop onto the hood of the novel. In this weird way, my lucky bullet came to my aid one last time by kicking off my career as a writer.

D. T.

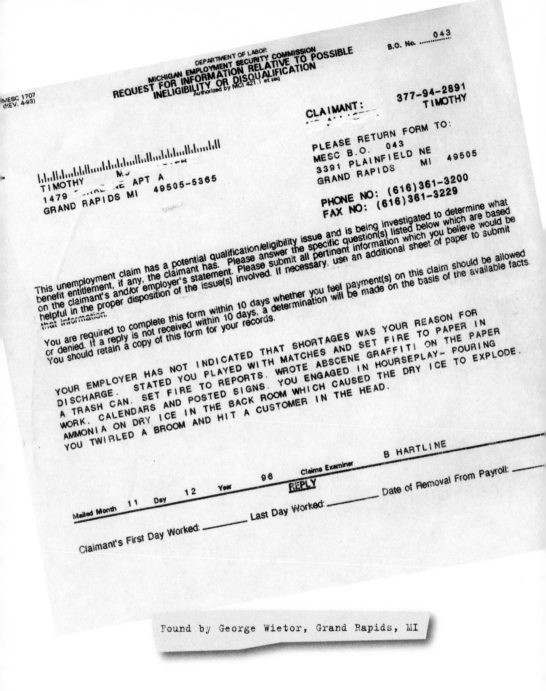

MESC 1707
(REV. 4-93)

B.O. No. 043

CLAIMANT: 377-94-2891
TIMOTHY

ılıllıdılılllındılıllılllındılılılılllıllındıll
TIMOTHY M........ER
1479 .... NE APT A
GRAND RAPIDS MI 49505-5365

PLEASE RETURN FORM TO:
MESC B.O.   043
3391 PLAINFIELD NE
GRAND RAPIDS   MI   49505

PHONE NO: (616)361-3200
FAX NO: (616)361-3229

This unemployment claim has a potential qualification/eligibility issue and is being investigated to determine what benefit entitlement, if any, the claimant has. Please answer the specific question(s) listed below which are based on the claimant's and/or employer's statement. Please submit all pertinent information which you believe would be helpful in the proper disposition of the issue(s) involved. If necessary, use an additional sheet of paper to submit that information.

You are required to complete this form within 10 days whether you feel payment(s) on this claim should be allowed or denied. If a reply is not received within 10 days, a determination will be made on the basis of the available facts. You should retain a copy of this form for your records.

YOUR EMPLOYER HAS NOT INDICATED THAT SHORTAGES WAS YOUR REASON FOR DISCHARGE. STATED YOU PLAYED WITH MATCHES AND SET FIRE TO PAPER IN A TRASH CAN. SET FIRE TO REPORTS. WROTE ABSCENE GRAFFITI ON THE PAPER WORK. CALENDARS AND POSTED SIGNS. YOU ENGAGED IN HOURSEPLAY- POURING AMMONIA ON DRY ICE IN THE BACK ROOM WHICH CAUSED THE DRY ICE TO EXPLODE. YOU TWIRLED A BROOM AND HIT A CUSTOMER IN THE HEAD.

Claims Examiner   B HARTLINE

Mailed Month 11 Day 12 Year 96   REPLY   Date of Removal From Payroll: ——

Claimant's First Day Worked: ——   Last Day Worked: ——

Found by George Wietor, Grand Rapids, MI

YOUR EMPLOYER

Nelly Reifler

Nelly Reifler is a writer and teacher living in Brooklyn; her collection of stories is called *See Through*.

"Your employer has not indicated that shortages was your reason for discharge. Stated you played with matches and set fire to paper in a trash can. Set fire to reports. Wrote abscene graffiti on the paper work. Calendars and posted signs. You engaged in hourseplay—pouring ammonia on dry ice in the back room which caused the dry ice to explode. You twirled a broom and hit a customer in the head." She fell. You stepped on the hand of the customer. She was lying on the floor. You ground the heel of your boot into her fingers—ring and pinky. Right hand. The damage to her bones was irreparable. They were no longer bones, according to your employer. Now they were dust, they were sand inside the pulp of her flesh. Your employer has stated that you turned off lights in back room. Dragged customer. You laid yourself down next to customer. She was whimpering. You put your mouth on her mouth. A block of dry ice evaporated nearby. The fog, undulating through beams of light cast by chinks in cinder-block wall of back room, was, you whispered to customer, "romantic."

YOUR EMPLOYER HAS MADE RECORD that you poured tight rings of hydrochloric acid on floor. You made visiting schoolchildren stand inside the rings. Told them it was a game. You poked them with broom handle. Locked teacher in back room. Tied her to drum of ammonia. Made her stand on cube of dry ice. Your employer has stated that you engaged in horseplay with schoolchildren. One of them cried. A little boy. "Hello, my name is Milo," his sticky name tag said. "Hello, Milo," you said. "Why are you crying?" "I'm scared," said little boy Milo. Sometimes children don't understand. They are little, need to be taught. "Are you a scaredy-cat, Milo?" you said. "A 'fraidy-cat? A yellow cat, Milo?" Your employer has reported that you laughed. You laugh through your nose. You squatted down and reached across the acid ring. Pinched Milo's cheek with your PVC glove. Milo wet his pants. Two schoolchildren were burned. Schoolteacher had seizure.

YOUR EMPLOYER HAS INDICATED THAT you like waterfalls. You like birds with black wings, you like dogs with long teeth. You like clean white cotton, you like brick chimneys. Your employer has indicated that you dream of your mother. Sometimes you are yelling at her, sometimes you are saving her. Your employer has evidenced that your skin is laced with scars. You like milk chocolate, rice pudding, clear broths. You like primary colors in small doses. You dream of places you've never been—they feel familiar, and you are always trying to arrive or escape.

YOUR EMPLOYER HAS AFFIRMED THAT you reordered the hanging files in comptroller's office. Instead of being alphabetical, the plastic tabs spelled out the name of your cousin, JANICE T. SOULY. Died of a virus. Hitchhiker. Streetwalker. Your employer has stated that Janice T. Souly, when young, lived with you and your mother. Sang to you, told stories, put you to sleep. You were little, needed to be taught. Janice T. Souly, when young, was pure and clean, like soap. Some soap is made from animal fat. Ammonia dis-

solves soap. Methamphetamine is commonly made from ammonia, pseudoephedrine, iodine. Ammonia is food for certain plants, such as hydrangea
and cucumber. Pseudoephedrine is used as a decongestant. What happened to
Janice? Was it your fault? Probably. Your employer has asserted that most things
are your fault.

YOUR EMPLOYER HAS NOT INDICATED that shortages was your
reason for discharge. You play with fire, burn paper in trash can. In order to be
forgiven, you must destroy. In order to be punished, you must do wrong. You
unplugged telephone in back room. You wrote obscene graffiti on dead customer's stomach. You held her crumpled hand in your hand. She grew cold. You
twirled a broom. You like dogs with long teeth, birds with black wings.

JENNY

POISON

EARTHQUAKE

FIRE

KILLING HIM

Richard Siken

Richard Siken, editor of *Spork* literary magazine, has freckles and likes Thai food. He would make a good boyfriend. You should call him.

JENNY

If he likes her so much she can do it. I could tell her things about him she has no clue she's not better than me she's not even a junior. She'll feel like me in a couple months anyway. I could befriend her and be on her side and help her rage against him until when he dumps her she can kill him and I'm so innocent. That picture of him on Facebook, I took that one. He's looking at me, at me that way not you. Jenny, nobody cares if you listen to NPR. And you don't. And chokers made out of shells look stupid. And you're stupid enough I could convince you to kill him even before he breaks your heart like he broke my heart and you would wake up in the middle of the night and stab him right in the futon where he lay. You're the one that was throwing up green beer all down the side of his Pontiac in the drive-thru and you were supposed to be my friend. He's not the only guy in a band, Jenny. You could have picked a guy in a different band. Balls.

POISON

I COULD INVENT A POISON THAT kills by touching but not kills right away and the antidote that I would have to drink first and then I could go to the bar and say enough bad things about Jenny that he would have to slap me and then later he would be dead. Or I could put the poison on my hand and slap him or on his guitar or better I could put it on his pool stick and he would stand there drinking Coors Light with his friends at the Bayhorse and he would go down hard and they would try CPR but too late they're also poisoned. One less local band so sad. Or I could mix the poison into my glitter lotion and then re-seduce him for grudge sex and make sure that the poison was not fast-acting so I could enjoy it and then pee on all his clothes and get out of there and find an alibi. When he's got his earbuds in and his iPod on he isn't thinking about you Jenny he's thinking about how to be a rock star playing gigs and singing the songs he wrote about me. About me, Jenny. And he looked better with long hair.

EARTHQUAKE

BE REAL NICE TO JENNY and convince her to move to San Francisco. He would follow her. They wouldn't know to stand in the doorway when everything shakes. Or I could seduce Jenny's brother and together we could get them hooked on drugs so when the earthquake hit they wouldn't realize it was an earthquake and then tragedy upon them. And you'd look like hicks before the earthquake so even if it took awhile for it to happen you'd be walking around with your weird tan lines acting like you know what a big city is like but you don't. You can't just change shirt styles in the middle of the summer. I lived in Dallas for almost a year. I wouldn't have a problem in San Francisco. I don't care if you have matching tattoos now the earthquake will crush you under its awesome rubble and no one will be able to see your tattoos and no one's gonna dig you out so they won't even be important in identifying the bodies so no one else will know either. Or care.

RAG IN THE GAS TANK or gas on the carpet no on all his things and the bar where he works downtown all of downtown I will set this whole ruined town on fire burning burning burning burning in a dress of red fury dripping flames an orange scarf nuclear orange blinding flames from my fingers laser-beam eyes I curse you all bow down before me and my destruction an enormous hell storm raging through the apartment complex the band's practice space the lacrosse field the sandwich shop or even Jenny's duplex I hate you Jenny I hate you and I'll look him right in the eyes and make him see how I was the best thing he ever had the best thing ever before I explode him into pieces with my stupendous fireball vengeance burn his lips his soft skin his brown shirt that makes his eyes so green his loose-fit jeans his Livestrong wristband you shouldn't have done me wrong like that burn and burn you shouldn't have left me I condemn you to endless fire why won't you love me anymore love me not her

THE GOOD PIRATE

Paulo Coelho

Paulo Coelho is author of the acclaimed novel *The Alchemist*.

hen I was a child, I was far more interested in hiding things than finding them. Like a good pirate, I had plenty of treasures to bury in my backyard. But these treasures were often things I'd found, like coins or shards of glass. Marbles were my preferred treasure. I would bury them in a little box in the yard, always close to a tree so that I wouldn't forget where I'd hidden them. One time I couldn't find the marbles I'd buried. I must have dug up half the yard looking for them. I would bet they're out there still. I think every child must believe that he or she has a secret treasure trove.

When I turned forty, I decided to make a pilgrimage to Santiago de Compostela. While there, I had an incredibly vivid vision that I was to become a writer. Of course I ignored this idea at first. People always end up postponing their dreams for the same few reasons: You think you cannot make a living following your dream, or your friends tell you that what you want is impossible to achieve. But the pilgrimage was a very powerful experience for me, and the urge to acknowledge the truth of my vision was a strong one. Still, I was on the fence about it all. A few days after I returned from Santiago de Compostela to

Madrid, I made a deal with myself. I said, "If I find a white feather tomorrow, I will take that as an omen that I should write a book."

The next morning, I left my apartment at around eleven o'clock and promptly forgot about the bargain I had made with myself. I spent the morning like most others, walking the streets of Madrid alone, taking in the sights and sounds of the bustling city. I must have stopped in front of this little café for only a moment, but that brief pause was all the time I needed to spot a beautiful white feather resting lightly on the ground.

I took the feather back to my place and immediately sat down and began to write. Those pages eventually became the opening pages of my first book—I achieved my dream of becoming a writer. Since then, every time I feel like it's time for me to begin writing another book, I wait to find a feather. Then, when I finish the manuscript for the book, I take the feather that inspired me to begin writing and touch it to every page before sending it to my publisher to be printed. When the first printed copy comes back to me, I put the feather attached to that book between its pages.

I believe in science. But there is something magical about finding things. People say of my feather ritual, "Oh, that's just superstition." No—superstition is black cats and salt over the shoulder. Finding things is different. The universe places things in your path; it's the language the universe uses to communicate with you.

I must have told the story of the feather once in an interview, because now I often receive white feathers by post. It's as if people think I have some Pavlovian response to feathers, that seeing them triggers me to think, *Oh! I should start writing a book!* I'm always pleased to receive them, but it just doesn't work that way. I have to find them myself.

D. T.

DIRECTIONS TO FINDING YOU (OR MAYBE JUST AN INFERIOR PRAYER)

Angel Nafis

Angel Nafis coaches the Ann Arbor Youth Poetry Slam Team and
performs her own work nationwide.

for my friend Maggie, after gifting her with a dead butterfly that I found

Say a butterfly had to die for you to get a gift

there must be some kind of prayer in that.

I want to know how you feel about capture

say I saw it there, that dead contraption of warmth and wing on the

> *sidewalk,*

and bent down to take it with my hands

the way most humans do

when I should have used my imagination or some other less selfish

> *device.*

And isn't it something that when wings are fragile or transparent, and

> *almost not there at all*

I only thought of you—

and of me sometimes too, but only when I am bleeding—and borrowed

> *them to write this poem.*

It was dead, but not without life.

And isn't it something that once I put it in the envelope and sealed with my tongue there was no turning back, or un-tasting of

the vinaigrette of loving you?

I've seen people misplace themselves in such a heart flare-up,

watched their temperatures drop,

and I don't know much about wilderness

but on days like these when you are harder to find,

I want to learn the word "seasons" properly

feel its backside roll against my molars

so I can feel free, like when we write to summon, or when you are far away

and I collect dead things to keep you alive in me.

Say hair that traps sky and gnats, say plash, say,

I could talk about the antenna or thorax

but I've already mentioned prayer and capture

and there's no turning back now—

the blood will come soon again,

say swish and slow movement, say

maps are irrelevant

say accidents are blessings too, say,

bellies of fish and coins,

say the texture of language,

hatching, and other raw things.

Say you accept this gift as all it was ever meant to be—

woman to search you,

say sister say this discovery of death and prism in my open fist.

Say sister say, this calamity of sweet and lack of coordination

and I am not afraid

of today, or an hour from now, or however long it may be

before someone captures my own dead butterfly self

off of some sidewalk.

I am here now,

speaking and giving

in bursts

of chest and effort, and temperature.

Illustration by Dan Tice, based on a photo found by Steve Almond

NO PANTIES ALLOWED

Steve Almond

Steve Almond is the author of two story collections, *My Life in Heavy Metal* and *The Evil B.B. Chow*, the nonfiction book *Candyfreak*, and the novel *Which Brings Me to You*, cowritten with Julianna Baggott.

My name is Rafer. I can't tell you my last name, for reasons that should become obvious. And I've had to change a few other things to tell this story, which, you don't have to worry, isn't going to be some long saga about how awful my childhood was because my dad was a scoundrel and my step-mom was a witch and my real mom died when I was five years old and *wah-wah-wah*. I'm just going to go over this crazy stuff that happened the summer between my sophomore and junior years.

I feel like I should mention up front that I like girls and that I've done girls. Not a lot, but enough, and I've had no problems doing them. I like the way they smell, the way they move, that sense they give you of knowing what a tool you are but putting up with it anyway. So the thing I'm going to talk about, it was more of a spontaneous thing.

"Circumstantial" is maybe the word I'm looking for, meaning tied to this one set of circumstances, or more like this one club that grew out of the frat, which wasn't an official club, just five or six guys who used to pile into the back of Pete Drury's pickup. See, Drury had lined the bed with a plastic tarp and filled it with water. Instant swimming hole.

Like I said, this was the summer after sophomore year and me and these guys had decided to stay on campus rather than going home. The college handed out jobs doing catering and shit, and they let us stay in our frat free of charge if we did caretaking stuff. It was a good deal, except that it was hotter than hell most days, like up into the high nineties, and so humid you felt like you were walking around inside somebody's mouth and the frat had zilcho AC because of some regulation.

We could have gone to this one state park with a river or used the pool at the gym complex. But you couldn't drink in those places, and that was a lot of why we liked Drury's pickup. Also because it was private, like a clubhouse almost, because he parked it in this patch of woods behind the frat, far enough away that the rent-a-cops wouldn't give us any hassle.

So that's what we did most afternoons: We'd grab a bunch of Busch and a plastic jug of McCormick mixed with OJ or cola and sit in the pickup and get wasted. There was me, Drury, Wilson, Maldo, Mahoney, and Finn, though he was a part-timer because he had the night shift at the student clinic. I was the youngest, the others were seniors, so it felt like a big deal to be included. Mahoney had been the pledge chair when I rushed. He had this squinty way of looking at you with his head cocked, like you'd just farted, and he was so handsome you had to convince yourself you hadn't farted. He was vice president now and Drury was secretary.

There was a lot of talk about girls. Who sucked cock and whether they spit or swallowed, and whether Tina Felton did or didn't have a cum jar under her bed. That argument went on for weeks. And sports, obviously. Everyone was a huge Braves fan, except for Wilson, who rooted for the Cards, or, as Drury called them, the Fagbirds.

One day we got into this big debate about which was more important: girls or sports.

Drury argued girls. "Blow job or night game? Come on."

Most of us were inclined to agree.

But Wilson, from under his visor, said, "Bullshit. I can jack it without a girl. That's a problem I can handle. But no Braves? Think about that."

"Think about Mariah Daube's ass," Drury said. "Think about her muff—"

"We're talking sports," Wilson said, real seriously. "No Hawks. No Falcons. No NASCAR. No brackets. Nothing."

"Girls," Maldo said. "Don't be a fagbird. Girls."

"Like you're getting any puss," Wilson said. "Your dick wouldn't know what to do if it smelled puss."

"Actually," Maldo said, "my dick isn't the size of a nose, like yours, so it doesn't actually smell."

"Enough dick," Mahoney said.

But the weird thing was, as he said this, his thigh came up against mine. Or maybe it wasn't that weird. There were six of us in that truck bed, lined up three on a side. But it felt weird to me, like a kind of private question.

Wilson and the others kept chewing on this question for awhile longer, but I could feel this swish in my gut and I glanced at Mahoney and he had that same squinty smile on his face, which didn't tell me anything, so I pounded the rest of my Busch and smashed the can against my forehead.

THAT WAS THE OTHER THING about Drury's pickup: We were fucked up so much of the time. We must have spent half our pay on booze. We were buying in bulk, very large quantities. So most of the time we were plastered and that only made us more reluctant to do the sorts of things that nonalcoholics do, such as eating solid food and drying out and sleeping regular hours.

Most days, we were in that pool from the time we got off work till after dark, because it felt like a special thing, like a frat within a frat, something we shared, a brotherhood. I'm sure most of the guys who stayed that summer had some version of the same fucked home life I did, though we didn't talk about that because there was other stuff to talk about about, such as how shitty our jobs were and how shitty our bosses were and how when we got out of school we were going to make a ton of money and what we were going to spend our money on and whether the Braves were going to chunk it in the playoffs again.

THE SKINNY-DIPPING THING GOT started when Drury invited these two townie chicks to tub with us. They were both pretty enough, even though one had snaggled teeth and the other had bad skin. But they were loud and kind of coarse and there wasn't enough room for everybody, so me and Finn had to bail into the cab and talk to everyone through that little window, like we worked at the fucking drive-thru. Anyway, at one point Drury says to these girls, "This is a no-panties zone, ladies." They started giggling and Snaggletooth looked at Drury and said, "Fine. Then take your fucking panties off, loser!" Everyone cracked up. And Drury took his shorts off. That was how it started. The girls turned to each of the guys until they were all buck-naked, then they took off their own panties, and their bras.

Now I know what this is sounding like—some kind of a *Penthouse* gang-bang scenario. But that's not what happened. It was just this awkward giggly few minutes, with the girls kind of sunk down so their tits weren't hanging out. Then one of them mentioned they needed to pee, so Drury took them into the house and Maldo came with and after a while it was clear they weren't coming back and me and Finn got out of the cab.

But before we could get in the pool, Mahoney said, "No panties allowed!" and Wilson backed him up, so we had to strip down. It was weird being naked in that water, so close to the other guys, where you could see everything beneath the surface. It felt like we were much younger, that giddy feeling when you skinny-dip for the first time, and whoever you're with, it's a trust issue—you have to give up a certain amount of pride, but you also get to unload some of your self-consciousness—and the net feeling is one of lightness and freedom, a kind of pale flickering.

We stayed that way for a couple of hours, naked like that, as the sun went down and the light through the pines turned golden, then pink, then blue. We kept drinking and taking pissers and talking shit. Mahoney was next to me when the dusk came in and I felt his thigh again and I wanted to look at him but I didn't.

AFTER THAT, SOMEONE PUT A note up on the back window of the cab: NO PANTIES ALLOWED, which meant—which we understood to mean—that nobody was allowed to wear clothes in the tub. And we abided by this in a way that was secret enough that nobody else knew what was happening but not so secret that it felt dirty. It wasn't like we were out there with raging boners, doing some big, aquatic circle jerk. It was much more a quiet agreement, a special rule.

These were guys—Mahoney and Drury especially, but also Wilson—who had porked half the chicks on campus. They had photographic evidence. But the feeling you had when you hung out with them at a party or one of the bars on College Hill, any setting where there were girls around, really, was that they were tense, ready to pounce, like hunters. We were all like that when girls were around. We flexed our muscles and twisted our mouths, like nothing mattered to us, like we were hard as rock, like they could chisel away at us for years with their questions and hopes and still not reach anything soft.

But in the tub, it was different. We were relaxed. There was no point in pretending. We let our guard down. Which is how it happened, I guess, this one night I'm thinking of, toward the end of summer. The Braves had played the Dodgers, beat them 5–2, and we'd listened to the game on Drury's radio, drinking the whole time and listening to Wilson tell lies about this girl he'd done back home, in Kentucky, who was legally blind, owing to a firecracker mishap, and who, to distract men from her blindness, had developed the capacity to do tricks with her lady parts.

It was nearly eight when we sent Finn to get us calzones from the Pirate's Cove, where we knew the manager (she had a massive crush on Mahoney), and by the time we were done with them, it was almost dark. Someone mentioned school. It was creeping closer; the maintenance guys had showed up, and the dorks who ran the frosh-orientation program. And we talked about how many guys we were going to rush and what we might do to them and whether it was worth banging frosh girls, given the hassles.

But for the most part we just sat sipping beers, not saying anything, not having to say anything, as the stars appeared. The radio was on and we sang along to "Hotel California" and "Life's Been Good" and then "The Boys Are Back in Town" came on, good old Thin Lizzy, and even though it was just another classic-rock retread, it sounded beautiful and rousing and it made us all feel nostalgic and sort of, I guess, tender.

This is when I felt Mahoney's leg come up against mine again, more certain this time, less of an accident, and very slowly I leaned against him, his shoulder, and then our hips were touching under the water and I looked around at the guys, then at the trees and the stars above the trees and this fragment of moon hovering there, and I felt a sense of absolute contentment, very powerful, but also very fragile, like a thing I'd been waiting for, without knowing that I was waiting for it.

I was holding my beer in one hand and my other was in the water and Mahoney's was there, too, and we pressed the backs of our hands against each other and flexed backward so we could rub the pruny pads of our fingers together and I closed my eyes and felt that same darting sensation, like some ancient fish had got loose in my gut. I wasn't thinking how I wanted Mahoney, or, *Oh, shit, I'm a faggot!* or any of those other things that I'd have imagined if you'd described the situation to me. I wasn't thinking anything, except that I wanted the summer to go on and for us to have this place where we could hang out together and feel whatever we felt, even if that feeling was the forbidden promise of another guy's skin against yours.

What I'm telling you is: I didn't want the moment to end. And if I did think about what this *meant* later on, it was only in the sense that I knew the moment *was* going to end and everything would snap back to the way it was the rest of the time, with Mahoney as our big alpha game hunter, loud and ruddy and lovely and mean, as required, and the girls who would always be around and would offer him whatever pleasures he could wring out of them, and those girls would be available to us, too, according to our efforts, but it would all be a sad compromise at the bottom of it, beneath all the flirting and heaving and sweat, because we could never be with them entirely, or they with us.

AND THAT WAS THAT. THE moment did end. The song ended and Mahoney jerked his body away from me, as if I'd been the one who started things, and Finn got up to fetch another beer and stepped on Maldo by mistake and Maldo kicked him over the edge of the truck bed and he cracked his eyetooth in the fall. So then the two of them were going to fight, naked like a couple of plucked chickens, but Mahoney and Drury told them to chill, we were going to drink a fucking toast to brotherhood, and they shouted at all of us until we got back in the tub and lifted our beers.

"There comes a time for good men to speak truth," Drury said.

"This is faggoty," Wilson muttered.

Mahoney's arm shot out and he snapped Wilson's visor with real violence. "What's faggoty?" he barked. "That we're brothers? That we made a fucking pledge to be brothers?" And he looked at me then, quick, as if to acknowledge something once and once only for the rest of time, his smile kind of glowing in the dark, and whatever hopes I had turned inward now, burrowed down to the place girls dream about and ask after and plead and nag for and only later come to realize doesn't exist at all.

Drury reached over and tousled Wilson's hair. Maldo let out a burp of terrifying volume. Finn punched himself in the face and started cackling. "Toast," I said. "Fucking toast it up, you naked motherfuckers."

THE JOURNAL PROBLEM

Jacob Slichter

Jacob Slichter is the drummer for the band Semisonic and the author of the book *So You Wanna Be a Rock & Roll Star*.

A few months ago, while rummaging through a storage box for a cassette tape, I found a pile of my old journals. I pulled them out and turned the small stack in my hand—a few of the black hardbound variety, a marbled black-and-white college notebook, a spiral-bound book with a floral design on the cover. I'd been avoiding these things for years, encountering them only when packing or unpacking moving boxes or looking for some lost item. With each encounter, deferring the decision to read or toss them seemed less defensible, yet holding them in my hand made me nervous. Was I really going to continue this game of hide-and-seek? Wasn't it time to make a decision, to sit down and read them or get rid of them once and for all?

THE JOURNAL-WRITING SEED WAS planted in the ninth grade when I went with my sister and parents to see *The Man Who Would Be King*, an action thriller set in the mountains of central Asia. The scene that captivated me the most was not any of the gun battles, avalanches, or palace riots depicted onscreen, but a quiet moment in which Rudyard Kipling, played by Christopher Plummer, hunches over his desk and writes in his journal. The sight of a pen dipping into an inkwell, the sound made by the nib scrawling across the page, the shapeliness of handwriting in the pre-ballpoint era—it all combined to leave me transfixed by the idea of keeping a journal myself. I loved the thought of ending up with all those beautifully inked pages, a physical object that would say, "I've been doing a lot of thinking." Onscreen, Kipling's squinting eyes fired out from behind his wire-rimmed glasses with the sort of blazing intent that ignites a literary classic. I leaned forward in my seat, trying on a fiery squint of my own.

But I did not get around to keeping a journal until the spring of my senior year in college when a couple of close friends stunned me with a blistering critique of my flagging political commitment. Why had I bailed on helping campus organizers stage a forum on racism? Was this an early sign of the postcollege, apolitical me to come? It sent me into a tizzy.

Feeling unjustly accused, I purchased a blank writing book, marched down to a park bench alongside the river at the edge of the campus, sat down, and began to write. An hour after my friends' harsh words, my fury had now metabolized into an amalgam of defensiveness, melancholy, and nostalgia. I started my journal with a few lines about loneliness, childhood, the sky: "Maybe it's hard for these East Coasters to understand someone from the Midwest. . . ." A noble passage of Aaron Copland's *Appalachian Spring* swelled in my mind as I wrote. As I pursued these themes, however, my attention was gradually overtaken by the vague awareness of a face, an imagined face suspended over the words, the face of the person expressing the thoughts on the page. I paused after a few paragraphs, when visions of that face became too much of a distraction.

I closed the book and started walking back to my apartment. My first journal entry—was it great? I wasn't sure. The more I thought about what I had written, the more I kept picturing the face that had emerged in my imagination as a result of writing. Something about it bothered me. The twinkling of the eyes seemed suspicious. The lifted brow strained for self-importance. As that face came into focus, I saw false innocence, smugness. I quickened my pace as

I recalled what I'd written. It wasn't great, good, or even mediocre—it was awful.

By the time I slammed and locked my apartment door, I felt like burning the journal right then and there. Throwing it in the trash was too risky. A stranger, maybe one of the tough guys next door, might read it. Hanging on to it was equally risky. My roommates might read it. *I* might read it. And yet as I paced about, I couldn't bring myself to set it aflame, rip it up, or otherwise dispose of it. It was as if some camp counselor had grabbed my shoulders and said, "You're only responding this way because you've been conditioned to find yourself embarrassing. You have to embrace the person who shows up on the pages of your journal. Someday, you may want to hear what he had to say." I was certain I never would. Nevertheless, the imagined counselor prevailed, and I hid my journal behind the tallest books on my bookshelf. In the following weeks, I peeked every so often to make sure it remained safely hidden. After graduation, I buried it at the bottom of one of my moving boxes.

That journal became a frightening object, damning evidence of the egotist within, someone who needed to be locked away lest he reveal himself to the world. When I unpacked my belongings in my postcollege apartment in San Francisco, I left the journal in its box, covered it with a baseball mitt and a can of once-used tennis balls, and stowed the box high on a closet shelf.

AFTER ONE DISASTROUS ENTRY, I'D had enough of journal writing. The only writing on my agenda was songwriting, the focus, along with drumming, of my rock-star ambitions. Alas, songwriting vexed me. I tried stoking my creative fire by reading books about liberation theology, U.S.-backed genocide in East Timor, and the civil rights movement. Then I sat with my pen and legal pad, waiting for the profound songs to arrive. They never did.

My roommate and close college friend, Dan, was a songwriter himself as well as a painter. As I stared at blank legal pads, writing a line of lyrics here and there and then scratching it all out, Dan cranked out song after song. And he made sketch after sketch and painting after painting. To top it all off, he was a devoted journal keeper. His freshman roommate had gotten him into the habit, and now Dan was sold. "It's amazing to go back and read some of those old entries!" he said. I shivered. As Dan scribbled away on our dining room table and the black journal books accumulated on his shelf, I envied the focus and self-possession that made his output possible.

Within a few years, both of us moved to Minneapolis. Dan had gotten married, and I had a growing list of friends and acquaintances who had recorded and released records, shown their art in galleries, and completed unpublished novels. Nearly all of them kept journals.

An artist friend of mine, battling her own creative demons, told me about a self-help book for blocked artists that she'd recently discovered. "One of the things it tells you to do is keep a journal. Every day!" I was suspicious. Nevertheless, I went to the bookstore, snuck in and out of the self-help section, bought my own copy of this book, and read it behind my locked bedroom door. The book spoke of the shame that stands in the way of creativity and the importance of getting past it. It rang true. I was largely embarrassed by the songs I had written, and I didn't like my singing voice. Why not have another go at keeping a journal? Leaving the old journal in its storage-box tomb, I bought another blank writing book and, as the self-help book recommended, began to write in it each morning.

The first week of this new journal-keeping routine surprised me. I enjoyed seeing the finished pages accumulate. I found myself writing down ideas for songs and other writing projects, sometimes writing for an hour or more. I felt I'd finally hit my creative stride.

As the routine continued, however, I once again began to form a vision of the face of the journal writer. At times he shaped his mouth into a pout: "Maybe the people at that party would rather have talked to someone who thinks about less important things. . . . If she could handle a serious-minded guy, she'd return my calls." Other times he waggled his brow in thinly veiled self-importance: "Of course, the songs would come easier if I could bring myself to adopt lower standards." The more I wrote, the more clearly I understood who I was seeing— a narcissist who cloaked himself in the mantle of the underdog, the kind who sits down with a friend and, after a few seconds of misty-eyed silence, draws a breath to say, "My new therapist says I have to start putting myself first."

After three weeks I'd had it. If the person singing on my homemade song demos was irritating, the guy writing my journal needed to be smacked in his smug little mouth. I closed this second journal for the last time and buried it next to its older companion in that same storage box, which was now doubly radioactive.

SOON AFTER ABANDONING JOURNAL NUMBER two, I teamed up with Dan and our mutual friend John to start a band. We played locally at first, then began to travel to clubs around the Midwest, and then the South and East. Part of our daily routine on the road included an hour or so of downtime in a coffee shop, where Dan would haul out his latest journal for a few minutes of purposeful scribbling. Town after town, show after show, Dan continued to rack up the journal entries. Not only did it remind me that his songwriting output continued to soar while mine sputtered, but it also made me wonder if perhaps being on the road might just be the perfect opportunity to take another crack at keeping a journal. I let that thought simmer, feeling cautious after two failed attempts.

Then, on vacation in London, I strolled past a window display of fountain pens and soon found myself under the spell of a pen salesman. After a brief analysis of my grip, he handed me a beautiful Parker. The tactile sense of the paper beneath the nib, the effortless flow of the words—writing had never felt so good. Our band had just signed a record deal, and buying a pen seemed like a perfect way to reward myself—maybe I'd write songs with it, I thought, or even, perhaps, start a new journal. When the salesman mentioned that Paul McCartney purchased his pens at this same shop, the deal was sealed.

Back in Minneapolis, in a new apartment, I fawned over my new possession, which could turn "juice / half-dozen eggs / tp" into something resembling poetry. For songwriting, the pen's powers were found to be somewhat limited. I resolved, however, to try once more to keep a journal. Thousands of miles of travel, rock shows in far-flung locales, record deals, recording studios—I had a two-year backlog of experiences to record.

My two previous journals were now buried underneath some sweaters in my bottom dresser drawer. There they should stay, I decided. I bought a new blank book and waited patiently for the right moment. I took my time, making intermittent entries. The process was often slowed by a twenty-minute search for my prized Parker followed by five minutes in the bathroom running water over the nib and a few minutes of doodling on a legal pad to get the ink flowing.

Armed with my new pen, I wrote once every week or so. Life had changed. The rising fortunes of my band made themselves apparent in the rising self-esteem of the journal keeper, whose face once again seemed to hover above the page. He who had once pouted with his lips—"I guess she can't handle a serious guy like me"—now cocked back his head—"She's nice, but I wonder if she could keep up." I shook him off only to see him reappear with a slight twist at the end of his lips as he speculated about a second career in acting. Entry by entry, the face of the journal keeper came into sharper focus, until his presence once again became unbearable and I threw this journal underneath my sweaters with the others.

 ITH EACH ALBUM, THE BAND toured farther and wider. I made other attempts. The blank books were now purchased in London and Paris. The face brought to life by those journal entries now wore the arched brow and thin smile of a wine connoisseur: "Maybe she'd teach me French. Then I could do interviews without a translator." The familiar pattern repeated itself: fancy blank book bought; handful of entries made (with cleaned and prepped fountain pen); vague unease with journaling self; persistence; horror; bottom of sweater drawer further crowded.

On the heels of even more success for our band, I took a second apartment in Brooklyn. With a new city around me, I tried other journal formats. One friend told me, "I spend fifteen minutes every afternoon writing down notes on some problem of interest." That seemed reasonable enough. Leaving out all of the personal recollections might keep self-disgust at bay. I bought a blank book with graph-paper pages (in case my brainstorms called for Da Vinci–like sketches) and jotted down ideas in the local coffee shop. "Book on American politics, red/blue state divide, and the cultural politics of race/gender/religion." The first few entries extended over several pages. Then that face. Again! Now he wore the feigned nonchalance of a guest author on *Charlie Rose*. As I took notes, I had the strange sense that the coffee drinkers around me saw everything. "That guy thinks he's the next big public intellectual." Another journal retired.

I **BOXED** **UP** **MY** **JOURNALS** before moving in with my fiancée, and in that box they stayed until we got married, several years later. Then came that day several months ago when I went looking for an old tape and happened upon them once more. Nearly twenty-five years of journaling held in my hand, not a word of it revisited since being written. To read or to trash? After fifteen minutes of weighing the options, I placed them on the bookshelf next to my desk, perhaps encouraging myself to finally sit down and confront what I had written. Would it be as bad as I had remembered?

I still haven't found out. From time to time I look at them and imagine many of the entries are perfectly harmless, long-forgotten incidents recorded in hilarious detail. But the worst lines are still burned into what might be called my shudder lobe—the part of my brain that contains memories of my worst moments, the stupidest things I've ever said, and close calls behind the wheel. Sometimes I think I placed those journals in plain view to remind me of what happens when bad tendencies go unchecked.

A **FTER** **YEARS** **OF** **BEING** **BOTTLED** up, I succeeded in writing songs for my band and then wrote a book about our tangled quest for rock stardom. Though sustaining a journal past the first few entries had proved impossible, writing a book, it turned out, was a different proposition. The detestable face that had hovered over the pages of my journals disappeared behind the imagined faces of my editor and an anonymous audience of book readers, who hovered over the pages of my manuscript, inspiring discipline and focus.

Meanwhile, I discovered a workable journal format: I copy favorite passages of whatever book I'm reading. It's a welcome opportunity to use my otherwise idle fountain pen. Best of all, I'm actually able to go back and enjoy the entries. A record of what I've read, I figure, counts as some kind of personal document. And the face conjured from the text on any given page belongs only to some famous author. The features are largely blank, the brow and lips barely sketched in. As I read through the entries, I imagine the features that might correspond to each author's voice—a clear-eyed stare, a playfully raised brow, a stern mouth. I reflect on the words as flickers of mimicry make their way across my face and I try on greatness for myself, leaving not a trace of evidence behind.

MONTHLY BUDGET

RENT	600.
CELL PHONE	50.
TELEPHOE	50
ELEC/Gas	45.
CABLE	60.
Bus/TAXI	60
FOOD	500.
LIQUOR	600 INCL BArs ($20.00 per DAy)
LAUNDRY	30
CRACK	600
ATTORNEY	250
MISC	250.
ASVINGS	100

TOTAL INCOME NEEDED $ 3195.00

YEARLE INCOME NEEDED $ 38,220.00

THE MAN WHO WAS NOT THERE

Chuck Klosterman

Chuck Klosterman is a journalist, a cultural critic, and the author of five books, including, most recently, a novel called *Downtown Owl*.

When we think about any specific piece of art, we usually think about one central question: *What does it mean?* Most of the time, trying to answer that singular question is the reason we're thinking about art at all. But this is not the case with found art, or at least it isn't when I look at it. Whenever I look at the individual things in *FOUND Magazine*, I find myself asking a different question: *Why would this possibly exist?* At the core, those queries are probably the same; they're both trying to deduce the motives of the artist. But the difference is that, with found art, there really isn't any motive to establish, beyond the fact that somebody who owns a Magic Marker is (a) on meth, or (b) insane, or (c) depressed and incredibly lazy, or (d) passive-aggressively quasi-violent (and possibly on meth). It is my experience that things that are lost are not meant to be found by anyone but the loser, which is why they are almost always interesting to people who don't care.

However, I sometimes suspect a few of the accidental artists who exist in this magazine are not crazy at all, and, in fact, are not even accidental. I have always thought this. Take a look at this artifact from *FOUND #3*, for example: It is a monthly budget for someone who cannot exist. There is simply no human like this. There is no crackhead in Minneapolis (or anywhere else) who writes a monthly budget *with a typewriter* and thoughtfully intends to put $100 into a savings account every single month. There is no crackhead spending $30 on laundry—if you smoke a lot of crack, you will wear the same shirt a couple of days in row (possible exception: Whitney Houston). Nobody predicts that they will need a lawyer. Nobody smoking $20 worth of coke every day would only allocate $20 for booze (they'd never get to sleep). And while the cable makes sense, a landline for the telephone is completely extraneous.

I would argue that the person who made this list is not real. However, I am not suggesting that Lea McKenny Willcox fabricated the document herself— I have no doubt that this piece of paper was actually found in nature and that some unknown weirdo really did type it up and release it into society. What I do not believe is that there's any person in Minnesota who (1) lives this way, and (2) thinks this way. Which brings me back to the aforementioned question I always dwell upon when I look at something in *FOUND Magazine* that is too awesome to be true: *Why would this possibly exist?*

In truth, I am not sure. I am not positive why someone would make up this kind of list and lose it on purpose (I suppose the only obvious explanation would be an unquenchable desire to get in *FOUND Magazine*). But here is what I suspect: There is someone in Minneapolis who really wants this kind of fictional person to subsist in reality. They want to believe that such a person is out there, or possibly—and somewhat inexplicably—that they *could be* this person, were they just a little more together or a little more fucked up. They believe that the archetype of a responsible, ambitious crack addict is a rational dream. I mean, who wouldn't want to meet this theoretical list-maker? He seems awesome: legally sensible, fiscally organized, clean, likes to party, easy to reach by phone, etc. He is the dream lost bohemian, fascinating to all those who do not know him. But that just happens to be everybody, because he's not there. I don't think the dude who made this budget is lost. He'll just never be found.

I WAS TORN FROM A BOOK

Kevin Sampsell

Kevin Sampsell is an author and editor and the publisher of Future Tense Books. His latest collection of fiction is called *Creamy Bullets*.

A young boy found me between cars in the church parking lot. Holding me with both hands, he carefully blew the dirt away. He folded me twice and stuck me in his pocket, then walked somewhere that was silent and full of trees. He took me out and unfolded me. He stared for a long time, his eyes darting off to the side and blinking. The upper-right corner was burned from a fire, the mark just a flicker from my face. The boy folded me up again, but this time added another fold. I was tight in his pocket for several days it seemed. I didn't know where I was.

I USED TO BE SNUG, inside a book. Warm. Surrounded, I'm sure, by other beautiful women.

I'm on my hands and knees, looking just above the camera's lens. Biting my bottom lip, I'm wearing a pair of black panties that fit too tight and a Cleopatra wig. My breasts touch the floor, just barely.

That's me. Page 65. This book, this retrospective of an early career, was kept in the library of a photographer. Her students looked at me and sometimes took me home with them. I noticed the different ways they looked at me. The men would nod at me in some vague way and paw me with their flat, dry fingers. The women were different. Sometimes they would point at me and laugh. A few of them would linger and stare.

THE **BOY** **TOOK** **ME** **OUT** of his pocket and moved me to his pillow. There was a tear in its seam and he put me inside. It was better there. I imagined I was a cloud and when his fingers would brush me, I wanted real skin and a shape. There's nothing more I wanted than to have hands. To put my fingers through my boy's fingers and to go under his covers with him. Yes, I started to think of him as "my boy." His eyes dreaming all sorts of things when he looked at me. I didn't care that he was so young. He was the only one who looked at me with awe.

We both wanted me to be real.

A **MAN** **ONCE** **LOOKED** **AT** me with loud, pounding music everywhere. He would look at another page sometimes, too. But he'd always turn back to me and bite his lip.

It would start off calm. And then his eyes would switch from a casual search to a look of business. His shirt would come off. The page would turn. I heard the click of his belt buckle, the sound of leather sliding through belt loops.

THE **BOY** **SHOWED** **ME** **TO** his sister and her eyes danced all around me. "Do you think she would like me?" the boy asked her.

"You shouldn't be thinking of this stuff yet," she said.

"Do you think Mom would kill me if she found this?" the boy said.

"Maybe," she said. She scowled at me and then looked at the boy. "Give it to me and I'll make sure she doesn't find out."

The boy folded me back up and told her to go away. I felt myself become a cloud again. I felt a wave of pride, like I was something to be fought over. Then a nothingness, then sadness.

I REMEMBER BEING RIPPED OUT. The man seemed so studious as he folded me back and forth in a careful straight line. His hand pulled me slowly out of the book. Meat coming off a bone. He held me up to the light and I felt limp in the air. He put tape on me and stuck me to a metal wall. There were pages from other books and magazines that had been torn out and stuck around me. It felt dirty and cold all around me, with a pungent smell of rubber and gasoline. The man wore glasses and overalls. He spent most of his time underneath a car, his legs stiff and sticking out, as if he were sleeping. The radio played voices, not music. Sometimes I heard laughing and I didn't know where it was coming from. Once in a while, the man would look at me like he was looking into a mirror. He'd take off his glasses and rub his eyes and smile. I must have reminded him of something good.

THE BOY'S MOTHER SAW HIM looking at me. It was late in the day, almost dark outside. The boy looked sick and half-asleep. He had stayed home from school. I was smoothed out on the pillow with shaky fingers. He took something out of his pocket. It was a school photograph of a girl. Her hair was a long swooping blonde wave that ended neatly just above the white border of the photo. Her mouth looked too full and experienced for her age. Her eyes were open wide, as if she had been startled. He placed this face gently on top of mine, positioned it so we might merge in his mind. I felt ashamed in that moment. But then his bedroom door opened and I was swiped away with his frantic hand. The two elements of his fantasy fell separately to the floor. His mother stood in the doorway, her eyes alarmed and recoiling. Her whole face grimacing. She turned and walked away quickly, as if she were being chased.

I TRY NOT TO THINK of the fire because fire means death. I remember his legs under that car and the heat suddenly everywhere. His legs did not move. I thought he would shoot out from under there like I had seen him do before. There were loud popping sounds and flames splashing like waves against the walls. The smell of burning flesh and metal. The man's work boots were flickering torches on the ends of his stick legs. One wall collapsed and a burst of smoke rushed to the sky. It was raining. Thank God for the rain. I blew up in the air for a moment, fluttering with a small lip of fire trying to eat me from one corner. When I settled on a patch of concrete, someone stepped on me and the flame near my head stopped.

THE BOY AND HIS FATHER had a talk about me. It was the first time I had heard his voice and it was unfamiliar, too loud for the house. I suspected that the father did not even live in this house. There was an uncomfortable tone to their talk. It sounded scripted, as if they feared the mother was listening on the other side of the door. The boy, *my boy*, told of how he found me but stopped short of saying why he kept me.

What does it make you think of, the boy's father asked.

I don't know, the boy answered without thought.

Let me see it, said the father.

My boy reached into his pillow and set me on the bed between them.

Is there any more in there? the father asked.

My boy shook his head and looked at his doorway. His mother was nowhere to be seen. The father took his glasses out of his shirt pocket and scooted closer to me.

Does this picture make you feel excited?

My boy looked at his father sideways, unsure of the question. The father's eyes stayed locked on me a little too long. It's not so bad, he finally said. He took off his glasses, slowly folded them into his pocket. Then he picked me up, folded me just as gently, hands shaking a little.

I thought I heard my boy starting to cry.

I was slipped back into the pillow.

The father's voice got softer then. It's okay, he whispered. It's okay.

I heard the father's heavy steps walk over to the door and close it.

I'll throw it away, my boy said.

No, no, no, said his father. There was a pause. Just hide it somewhere else, he finally said. Don't let your mother find it. I'll say that I took it.

Really? I heard the boy wipe his tears, his drippy nose.

They talked awhile longer until the mother knocked on the door. Okay, said the father, I'll see you later. He left his son's room and talked to the mother in another room.

My boy took me out of the pillow. He unfolded me and gave me a look that was more guilty than I'd seen from him. He walked me to a wall and quickly took down one of the smaller posters. With a piece of tape he stuck me to the back of the poster and returned it to the wall. It felt good to be unfolded and safe. He stood there a moment and inspected the poster to make sure I wasn't visible. I heard him sigh loudly and then his bedroom light went dark. I knew it might be a long time before I saw him again.

Approaching Progress

Jonathan Lethem

Jonathan Lethem is author of eight novels, including *Motherless Brooklyn* and *The Fortress of Solitude*.

One afternoon about twenty years ago I went to a few dusty thrift stores in Berkeley, shopping for a manual typewriter. At this point, I was working in total isolation—I wasn't a published writer yet; I had no money; I worked at a used-book store. Everything I owned was secondhand at best, or found in an alley. The furniture in my house was all dragged in off of various curbs. There wasn't an object in my life that I had bought new. I figured an old manual typewriter would fit very naturally into my life.

At the last thrift store of the day, I finally spotted one and hurried over to examine it. It had a powerful dent on one side, as though it had dealt once or twice with the business end of a Louisville Slugger, and its old cloth ribbon was faded and fraying. A piece of paper was rolled into the carriage. This wasn't unusual; most stores selling old typewriters insert a piece of paper so that customers can type things like *The quick brown fox jumped over the lazy dog*, or whatever phrase they might be inspired to write to test the thing out. I always love taking a peek at these. Most commonly, you'll see typed lines like *Krystal loves Rick forever and ever*, or *This dam thing dont work does it*, or that strange, musical pair, *Qwertyuiop asdfghjkl*. On this particular piece of paper, though, there was typed just one sentence. I haven't laid eyes on it in ten years, but I have no hesitation about its exact wording: *You cannot approach progress by dweeling on fus.*

EVERYTHING WAS SPELLED CORRECTLY UP until the "dweeling on fus." No punctuation, all lowercase letters. The line looked tentative and almost heartbroken. The sentence had obviously fallen short of whatever its author had desired it to be. "Dweeling" and "fus" seemed clearly like pathetic, half-assed attempts at other words. But it's a strange sentence even before you get to "dweeling" and "fus." Because, of course, you cannot *approach* progress. "Dweeling" might hint at "dwelling," but then where was "fus" going? How much more was this person going to say before they just gave up? And the fact that they left the paper in the typewriter but didn't buy the typewriter? It's like everything just broke down. It's a conundrum that you could ponder forever. That's what I loved most about the line—you simply couldn't know what the writer was trying to get at. The whole sentence just crumbled into the void. Maybe if whoever typed it had found a way to finish the sentence, things could have gone differently for them. If they'd bought the typewriter, the page would have disappeared, but perhaps they would have realized eventually that they could bear to continue typing.

THE PAGE HAD AN UNQUESTIONABLE Beckett-like quality. In his letters, Beckett used to say of his writing, "I can't go on, I must go on." The man was unbelievably sick and tired of writing, yet apparently not sick and tired enough to stop. He continues by saying, "To write is impossible, yet apparently not yet impossible enough!" It's as if Beckett is apologizing for continuing. Obviously, the Beckett line is a lot more constituent than "You cannot approach progress by dweeling on fus." But in some ways, I felt like I had found a piece of street-Beckett. There is the absolute brokenness of any attempt to communicate, and yet, to me, it still communicated.

I found the enigmatic sentence to be an incredible piece of advice and wisdom. Though it's absolute gibberish, the line stuck with me. It became its own embodiment of the unapproachability of progress. I began to actually think of it as a piece of secret advice that was specifically meant for me, a mantra to default to when I was in need. When I'd wrestle with something, I'd say to myself, *Well, you know, "You cannot approach progress by dweeling on fus!"* The words tattooed themselves on my brain, an epigraph that the world had bestowed upon me.

AS A STRUGGLING WRITER, I'D rely on the world to throw me these kind of lifelines. Everything around me had a meaningful providence. At the time, this grimly tattered bit of thrift-shop wisdom epitomized the state I was in. After all, hadn't I been "dweeling on fus"—whatever that meant, exactly—for months now, even years? The idea of any communication that might be a clue or signal from the void was intensely charged for me. I don't think I bought the typewriter that day, but I do know that I snagged that piece of paper.

CHRISTMAS TED

Anna Stothard

Anna Stothard is a British novelist, journalist, and screenwriter; her first book is called *Isabel and Rocco*.

I gripped my father's hand as he tugged me through the Las Vegas cavalcade of ringing slot machines, arranged shoulder to shoulder on either side of us. In front of each machine, adults sat on swivel chairs that grew up out of a geometrically patterned carpet. It seemed absurd to me that there were so many grown-ups in this plastic fantasia. What were they doing pouring coins into the mouths of those gaudy machines? Why were they silently watching a little ball rattle around on a spinning circle? Why were they carrying coins in multicolored buckets?

Dad and I made our way toward the concierge desk. We'd spent the last hour looking for my four-year-old brother's lost teddy bear among the jumble of casino floors. Dad always walked fast and I was in the petulant habit of leaning back on his hand to slow his pace, physically reminding him of my presence at every step. Dad seemed oversized and remote in those days, like some sort of walking corduroy tree or a curious species of animal that I couldn't get a handle on and consequently felt ambivalent toward.

I think he was equally perplexed by me: this eight-year-old curly-haired creature with sticky hands and a nervous laugh. It wasn't that we didn't get on, it was more like we hadn't found common ground yet. I had a covenant with Michael, my brother, based on providing words, sweets, and information that he wasn't meant to have, and an intimate pact with Mum forged from eight years spent daily in her company, but Dad and I didn't share much that was exclusively ours. I wanted his approval, but had no idea how to get it. He was a journalist, a book collector, and an ancient-language enthusiast. I was an eight-year-old girl with a penchant for soccer and *My Little Pony*. We rarely did things without Mum or Michael around, and were somewhat shy when left alone together.

I pulled back on Dad's hand to stare at a grinning old man in a wheelchair who bathed his hands in a silver avalanche of coins cascading from a slot machine into the protruding metal lip underneath. Behind the old man lurked a huge plastic sculpture of a purple dragon, open-mouthed and gargantuan, part of the casino's pastiched medieval theme. Beyond, fake stone arches bore airbrushed scenes of wizards, knights, and demure, wide-eyed Guineveres.

I struggled free of Dad's engulfing hand, and for a moment he looked stricken, ready to grab at me, believing, perhaps, that I was going to dash off after the purple dragon, but instead I skipped forward toward the mammoth concierge desk and let loose a torrent of words at the stiffly dressed woman who stood at attention behind it: "Have you seen a teddy bear please we've lost him?"

The bear was known as Christmas Ted, its sweater emblazoned with a tinseled tree. I wanted to find Christmas Ted as much as Dad did—he'd become central to our family's dynamic that summer. Ted had voices, moods, opinions, all concocted by my mother, I've realized in retrospect, to manipulate Michael into happiness. Michael was a very careful, responsive four-year-old, who had an uncanny knack for picking up on other people's emotions. He later became an extremely talented poker player, presumably because of this sensitivity, and perhaps as the result of his early introduction to Vegas casinos. Christmas Ted was the love of Michael's life. Ted had an embroidered cotton nose and a mouth shaped into a wide O. His black marble eyes were sewn into his head at a jaunty angle, giving him an expression of perpetual nervous energy. He wore a vivid red knitted sweater, which was slightly frayed at the green-hemmed edges, and covered with souvenir badges from tourist destinations we'd hit that summer: a museum in Yosemite National Park, a diner on Route 66, and a gift-shop silver badge of a redwood tree silhouetted against a setting sun.

"Well," the lady behind the concierge desk replied humorlessly, "nothing's been handed in."

"Is there a lost-property room in the casino?" Dad asked.

The woman eyed him sharply, as though he was a guy who'd wandered onstage at a Shakespeare play and asked Hamlet directions to the restroom. Searching for lost property was apparently vulgar—perhaps in such a present-tense city devoid of clocks, the idea of lost property implied a past or future that nobody wanted to concede. I imagined a dungeon where they kept the lost souls of all those sad-eyed people stationed at the slot machines.

"Downstairs, maybe," the concierge suggested at last. "Basement floor, on your right, I think." Dad tried to take my hand again, but I snatched it back and strode off toward the elevator.

"Please don't be difficult," Dad said to me with a sigh.

"'Course not," I replied haughtily, deflecting his gaze.

We were becoming increasingly edgy, thinking of the tears and the horror that would ruin the rest of our holiday if Christmas Ted couldn't be found. Dad and I went down the elevator to a dank basement hallway with a speckled plaster ceiling and egg-colored walls. The carpet was the same pattern as in the loftier corridors, but worn into brown bristles and thick with the smell of stale cigarette smoke. There were no signs, but after several wrong turns we found a door marked LOST AND FOUND and stepped through into a large, uninhabited storage room. Streaks of sunlight—perhaps the only sunlight in the casino—strained down through the windows and lit up little galaxies of hanging dust.

Dad hit the light switch, and the pinkish fluorescent bulbs overhead revealed a scene unlike anything I'd ever seen before or have ever seen since. The room was vast, the size of a hockey rink, filled with an endless treasure trove of lost toys and broken costumes. There was a feathered, sequined leotard and two wedding dresses hanging from the ceiling, a mosaic salad bowl brimming over with car keys, a pair of crutches, a row of lonely single shoes, and a thousand dolls of every conceivable size. There were limbless and naked Barbie dolls, like an army of Venus de Milos; there were rag dolls with missing eyes; worry dolls the size of rice grains; and floppy Cabbage Patch Kids with cottony stuffing spilling from their ripped knees. I felt sick with excitement at the sight of this magic chamber, and Dad looked equally amazed, but neither of us could see Christmas Ted. There were other teddy bears, sure—one with a button-down jacket, one with his own felt suitcase and top hat, and dozens more—but not *our* Ted. Dad's face fell. So did mine.

"I guess we'll try again tomorrow," Dad said. We were about to turn and leave when I saw a worn brown paw sticking out of a rainbow-colored beach bag perched on a high metal shelf. I wouldn't have noticed it except that Michael always held Ted's left paw and the right paw was worn from often being dragged along pavements and carpets. I walked over to the bag and looked up.

"Up there." I pointed.

"That's not our bag," Dad replied.

"*Inside* the bag," I said. Dad reluctantly lifted me up from under the arms to let me pluck down the bag from its shelf. Sure enough, inside the bag, limbs akimbo, squeezed between a Nevada guidebook and a disposable waterproof camera, was a befuddled-looking Christmas Ted.

"Well done, Anna!" Dad shouted with genuine excitement. He kissed me, his beard tickly. I grinned at the pleasure of success and the thrill of being kissed. I also noticed that his eyes were exactly the same color as mine.

Dad and I went for celebratory milkshakes. We'd saved Christmas Ted from the macabre world of Vegas Lost Property, and I remember sitting opposite Dad, feeling utterly content, knowing that he couldn't have found Ted without me.

Later that night, Mum joined us back at our hotel; she held Ted affectionately on her lap. "Where'd you find him?" she asked.

"Anna found him at the Lost and Found." Dad shrugged, as if there was nothing of note about the lost property room.

For a moment I felt stricken; perhaps, I thought, the experience hadn't been as magic or memorable for Dad. I looked nervously up at him. Then, for the first time ever, he winked at me. The Lost and Found room was our secret.

And all that is left of her soldier boy true,
Are his sword and his cap and his red, white, and blue

POST CARD.

and all that is left
is his $1.00
Umbrella. and
it stops raing
What you are

Th. E., L. Theochrom. Series No. 1121   Prin

Found by Robert Olen Butler

THE ONE-DOLLAR UMBRELLA

Robert Olen Butler

Robert Olen Butler has written three collections of stories, including, most recently, _Had a Good Time: Stories from American Postcards_. He is also the author of ten novels and was awarded the Pulitzer Prize for fiction in 1993.

To Lydia Jones, I was doing swell, wouldn't you say? With all the hoopla in the street—the marching flags and the bands playing "Over There" and the conscripts passing in straw boaters—and you were stunningly emancipated with your hair rolled up high on your head and without a hat, and I stood staring at the back of your neck, which you had laid bare in your equality, and I was too weak to move from the sight of it. But I knew, didn't I, I knew what you were thinking as I finally stepped alongside you and I said, "If Woodrow wants to fight this war so badly, he should let you vote, don't you think?" and no fellow innocently on the mash ever has been blessed by the gods of eloquence as I was at that moment. You turned to me and I knew from your eyes I'd done swell even before you touched me on the forearm and bent near and shouted above a passing band how absolutely right I was. And we knew to walk off together, up Fifth Avenue at the back of the Liberty Bonds crowd, and we talked about how the world had gone so wrong, for women, for all of humanity, for America—abroad, we were fighting a war; at home, we were prosecuting dissenters and persecuting German Americans—and we were so very happy worrying together, you and I. Then it began to rain. And I knew the thing to do.

Ahead was a shop, and I pulled you into the doorway and I said to wait, and a few moments later I guided you back to our stroll. In my hand was a new umbrella, and I opened it up and put it over you. And as your hand clasped—equally with mine—the boxwood handle with military tassels, my eloquence turned to folly. "So you won't melt," I said. O my fiercely emancipated Lydia Jones, who art no lump of sugar in need of protection by a man, you then spoke a few words that I'd never heard a woman speak, and you dashed away into the rain, I'm afraid forever, and there is nothing left of me here. Not even my umbrella, which you took.

ROD AND FRANK

Ben Greenman

Ben Greenman is an editor at the *New Yorker* and the author of three books: *Superbad, Superworse,* and *A Circle Is a Balloon and Compass Both.*

You are about to enter another dimension, a dimension not only of sight and sound but of temper and incivility. A journey into a wondrous land populated by two men, each trying to get his hands around the neck of the other. Next stop, the Twilight Zone!

You are looking at Rod Serling, a student at Antioch in Yellow Springs, Ohio. You are also looking at Frank H. Thompson, Jr., another student at Antioch. It is 1958, and the two young men are standing in a hallway, talking. Behind them on the wall is a clock. The second hand is ticking. All of a sudden it starts to spin faster, and then faster still, and the two men beneath the clock, Rod Serling and Frank Thompson, begin to change. Their shoulders broaden. Their brows thicken slightly. They are aging, you see, as the clock rushes forward through time. Rod Serling becomes famous. He writes a script called "The Time Element," in which a man from 1958 is sent back to 1941—December 6, to be more precise—and consigned to an existence where he wakes, warns his neighbors about the impending attack, is ignored, sleeps, and wakes again in the same day. It is a cross between *Pearl Harbor* and *Groundhog Day*, and it propels Serling to great fame as the creator of a television series about similar strange plots and situations.

Frank Thompson, on the other hand, does not become as famous. In fact, as the clock spins forward and his shoulders broaden and his brow thickens, he begins to fade out, and by the time the clock reaches the early sixties, he has disappeared completely. It is as if he never existed.

And then, out of nowhere, Rod Serling, working hard and earning great rewards in the television business, is at home in Pacific Palisades when he receives a letter. The name on the return address sparks a distant memory. He opens it with interest. The writer is his old acquaintance Frank H. Thompson, and he is appealing to Serling, not just for advice about how to break into the writing game, but for money. "The only way to make it from good work to good and salable work is to be single-minded and selfish, I've discovered," writes Thompson. Serling writes back with a mix of tough talk and slashing dismissiveness. He lands several blows. Thompson, his ego bruised, replies. And the correspondence, already a wounded thing, stumbles on. To say more would interfere with the pleasure of reading it. These letters were discovered, along with other Serling correspondence, in a manila folder on the floor of a city bus in Madison, Wisconsin, by Davy Rothbart's brother Mike. They ran in Issue #4 of FOUND, which is where I found them.

The correspondence is not easy comedy. It's prickly and complex, with a number of tight turns and all manner of histrionic chicanery. Serling wants to play the role of Rod Serling, successful writer, as Thompson points out, but he also does not want to be targeted as an easy mark for flatterers. As Davy Rothbart pointed out in Issue #4's introduction, readers are likely to be split on the question "Who's the jackass here?" For my purposes, there was one question that lodged sideways in my throat, fish-bone style, as I read. What became of Frank H. Thompson? Did he slink away into obscurity? Did he get his precious money? Did his stories start to sell, as he thought they might, or did his possibly illusory muse desert him? I decided to find out.

The Serling-Thompson correspondence is dated 1965. That was the starting point, the first clue. As it turns out, it was also the only clue. I set out to see if I could find an author named Frank H. Thompson, Jr., publishing in the late sixties. I found one. He was the author of a number of books: *1984, Animal Farm, Jude the Obscure*. Pay dirt! This was a huge victory, and I celebrated for about an hour before I came back to earth with the realization that Thompson could not have written *1984* or *Animal Farm* or *Jude the Obscure*—at least not outside the Twilight Zone.

Further research solved the mystery. Thompson had not written those books but rather had written the CliffsNotes for them. CliffsNotes, of course, is the series of study guides to great works of literature: They summarize the plot, illuminate major themes, and generally permit junior high and high school students to watch *Gilligan's Island* rather than read the assigned course work. Now I was excited. The Frank H. Thompson, Jr., who had written to Serling had taught college English for eleven years before trying his hand at fiction. The CliffsNotes author in question was sometimes listed as "Frank H. Thompson, Jr., M.A." It had to be him. And then geography clinched it. Serling's old college friend was writing from his home in Lincoln, Nebraska. CliffsNotes were created by a man named Clifton K. Hillegass, a native of Rising City, Nebraska. In 1958, Hillegass learned of a Canadian series of study guides called Coles Notes, and with the encouragement of Jack Cole, he began to publish an American version of the series from his basement in Lincoln, Nebraska. The series was an instant success. In 1965, following the death of Jack Cole, Hillegass learned that he could no longer republish Coles Notes under the CliffsNotes name, and so he was forced to create a large number of new books. Frank H. Thompson, Jr., it seems, was a beneficiary of that demand. This is circumstantial, of course. It wouldn't hold up in court. But as a footnote to a show about strange coincidences, it flies.

Did Thompson continue to write to Serling? Did he make any real money from his CliffsNotes? Did Serling eventually make peace with his old college classmate? No one knows, and by "no one," I mean me. But I do know something else, and it's at least as interesting as the CliffsNotes to *1984*, in which we learn that George Orwell's totalitarian future state was meant to reflect the realities of his own times. The year after the correspondence with Frank H. Thompson, Jr., Rod Serling wrote a TV movie called *The Doomsday Flight*, which starred Ed Asner, Van Johnson, Edmond O'Brien, and Jack Lord. It's not a distinguished movie, exactly. It's said to be one of the inspirations for the *Airplane!* series, and one of the more waggish comments on Amazon.com reads, "The plane is going to crash . . . and so is Lord's career." It didn't, of course. Lord went on to fame as Detective Steve McGarrett in *Hawaii Five-O* just two years later. But Lord's character in *The Doomsday Flight*, a special agent, is named . . . Frank Thompson.

Cue spooky music.

Dear ~~Tommy~~• Alex,
If you don't give me
your brain ~~B~~ right
now then bring
$20 to the front

desk Now!!!

don't include the

Police.

DON'T INCLUDE THE POLICE

Aimee Bender

Aimee Bender is the author of three books: *The Girl in the Flammable Skirt, An Invisible Sign of My Own,* and *Willful Creatures*. She teaches creative writing at the University of Southern California.

ear Tommy,

I wrote Alex instead of you. I want his brain instead of yours. I got all antsy about it. Originally I loved your brain the most but then you said the thing about how the world is made of people's dead bodies, piled on top of each other, and how we were all just walking on bones and bugs all the time. I almost threw up. Alex's brain is better, because he talks about nothing. Once I went on a walk with him to Smart-Mart and we talked the whole time and I could not tell you one word of what we talked about!! If he brings me the $20 instead, Janet and I are going to the store right after school to get some gummies. We're going at three if you want to come.

PS: if you include the police I will tell them what you said about stealing Boffie's car.

Dear Tommy,

Did you get my other note? I left it at the front desk, in your box. Did you get it? Are you avoiding me? The store sucked. All the gummies were so old. They didn't even stretch. Janet called them oldies. I want your brain now. Big-time. Alex brought me his brain so I didn't have $20 anyway and his brain? It's bad. I held it and I felt like I was going to die of boredom. And I think he maybe included the police anyway. What am I supposed to do? I put it in the refrigerator. I was wrong about the dead bodies thing. You are right! There are dead bodies everywhere anyway! Like right here, in my refrigerator!

Dear Tommy,

Where are you?

Alex's brain is smelling up all my yogurts.

Did you take Boffie's car? Are you on the road right as we speak? I asked Mrs. Dobbins at the front desk if you'd looked in your box and she said it was still full of stuff. I feel so bad that I didn't ask you first. I meant to. You can see the cross-out, how I meant to.

Dear Tommy,

Hi. I gave back Alex's brain. Tad said it was no big deal and to give it back to the front desk and they would deal with it. He said they're used to it. Mrs. Dobbins gave me a look (was I supposed to put it in a paper bag? Do you know?) because of the refrigeration factor and she gave me no cash *at all* and she said Alex used to be a very nice young man and I had handled it all very poorly. Alex was drooling in the corner. He looks really bad. I asked her about the police part and she shrugged and said maybe they were on their way right that minute and you can't mess around with people like how I do. She said I had been rash. Rash? Is that a word? Like the itchy thing?

I think you're probably in Wyoming by now. I miss you.

Dear Tommy,

One last thought. I'm scared of thieves. Please put the lock on the zipper when you sleep. Please? You can get someone else to fasten it for you if you can't reach. I just don't want another girl to get it, okay? I'm sending this to your dad's address. I will stop writing after this. I think of you every night and I apologize to the air and I hope it will get to you somehow. Please accept my apology. They gave Alex a new brain yesterday and it was an astrophysicist's and now everyone is in love with him and asks him to explain everything. It all worked out okay, T. Please come home.

PERSONETTE

Kevin Dole 2

Kevin Dole 2 is a writer living in Ypsilanti, Michigan.

Things that I've found that have led me to judge their imagined owners:

- Soiled panties, paired with a used condom, in an abandoned parking lot

- A 20-year A.A. chip, on the sidewalk next to shards of a broken bottle

- A clean, functioning electric fan, on the curb with someone's trash

It was hard not to find things like this where I lived. A small, economically depressed Midwestern college town called Ypsilanti: a little bit country, a little bit postindustrial blight. It had its nice areas but I was in the part of town where the student ghetto overlapped with the regular ghetto. The kind of neighborhood where you'd find ripped-out hair extensions in the grass.

I found Personette's bag on the front porch of a boarded-up house as I was walking home from work one day. It was the style of leather tote that young professionals sling over their shoulders to indicate that they're young professionals. Someone had gone through it pretty thoroughly and the innards had spread as far as the sidewalk. Papers, mostly.

I tried to ignore them but the embossed state seal on the title to a car made me pay attention. I knelt to pick it up and my hand came away brown and sticky. I carefully sniffed, then tasted the streaks on my fingertips: chocolate sauce. I found the bottle it came from in the bottom of the bag, stuck to a welder's mitt. The bottle was small and made of thick glass, like a vial of perfume. The label showed the shapely back and shoulder blades of a nude woman.

Clearly, it was all important stuff, so I gathered up everything and took the bag back to my apartment.

My girlfriend couldn't wait to look through it. I wanted to also, but felt that I shouldn't, so I pretended that I didn't want to. She resolved this dilemma for me by reading some of the choicer contents aloud, excited enough by the find to ignore the fact that I clearly disapproved and was doing my best to look down on her for pawing through someone else's possessions. I ended up going through the whole bag anyway once she'd gone to sleep—just to find the owner's contact information, I told myself.

Personette was his last name. He was a couple of years younger than I was, earlier in his twenties. His whole life, writ small, was in that bag. It was a dossier, the kind people pay private investigators to put together. Along with the car note, I found:

- A citation for possession of marijuana, which was in violation of his probation

- An accompanying note verifying that he had attended at least one meeting of Narcotics Anonymous

- A threatening letter from a credit agency

- A class schedule at a local community college

- The syllabus for a welding class at said community college

- An eviction notice from an apartment complex

- A note to his daughter's kindergarten teacher about the recent change in her last name to something other than Personette

- A neatly typed, poorly written letter to a local court explaining to the judge his reasons for starting a fight with his ex-girlfriend's new boyfriend on their front lawn, and exactly why that didn't constitute assault

At the bottom of the bag was a plastic, accordion-style file folder in which the papers had once, presumably, been carefully arranged. Maybe his assembling of them that way was a vain attempt to get his shit together. I wondered if it had brought him satisfaction to file them like that, to bring the appearance of order to a life that seemed so clearly out of control.

His only listed address was the complex that had kicked him out. His phone number, if he had one, wasn't on any of the documents. But his mother's was. He had cited her as a character reference on some legal paperwork.

I called her the next day. She was confused at first, but seemed relieved when I explained the situation. She hadn't known anything was wrong, but was glad to learn that it was on its way to being fixed. She gave me Personette's cell number, prefaced by the same long-distance area code as hers.

I got his voice mail but he called me back the same day. It turned out he was staying with a friend in town, just around the corner from the house where I found his stuff. The bag had been lifted from his van, which was parked in his friend's driveway.

I suggested that we meet at the library, which was about halfway between us. He asked if it was near the local strip club. It wasn't far. I tried to give him directions by referencing other landmarks, but the strip club worked best. We agreed to meet in front of the library.

Standing on the steps, I thought about my brother, who was about the same age as Personette and had similar troubles with the law. I thought about the single, awkward time that I'd attempted to use chocolate sauce as an erotic accessory. I thought about how I'd told my girlfriend about the former but would never tell her about the latter.

I thought about the apartment complex that had evicted him and the people I'd known who'd lived there. I thought about the people I knew who went to the community college. I thought about how I used to ride the bus past both those places regularly. Maybe I'd seen him before.

I hadn't. But even before he called out my name, I could tell it was him by the purposeful way he approached me. He was big. I'm not short, but he was taller than me and broad through the shoulders and chest in a way that made me feel small. He wore fashionable glasses, hipper than mine, that looked small on his head, a kind I wouldn't have imagined on a welder. His handshake was firm, his gaze direct. He was casually affable, but businesslike. He could have been trying to sell me a used fishing boat.

He must have known that I had gone through his papers. How else would I have gotten his number? I had spoken with his mother and knew the name of his estranged fiancée. I knew his daughter's name, and that he and his ex had fought over it. I knew the number of his probation officer. I knew every sordid detail of his existence that could conceivably end up as a matter of public record. I knew that he owned—and had presumably used—erotic chocolate sauce.

He had to know that I knew these things. Yet he seemed to feel none of the shame that I would have felt in his place, nor any of the kind that I felt at that moment. I had laughed at him behind his back, but meeting him face to face, I felt like a lesser kind of person.

On paper he was a mess, but in the flesh he was confident. Upbeat. Clearly less worried than I was. Maybe he didn't see any reason to feel ashamed. Maybe he was just glad to have his stuff back.

On paper my life looked great. Or at least better than his. After a few years of marginal employment and temporary homelessness, I had my first real, post-college job. I had a salary. Benefits. A 401(k). No debts to speak of. I lived in a nice flat above a shop downtown with a beautiful woman.

But the job overwhelmed and depressed me. And the woman, though I loved her passionately, confused and exhausted me more than anything else. We fought constantly. Most of the time—including that moment, standing on the library steps, shaking Personette's hand—I was a nervous wreck.

He wasn't.

"Hey, man, I really appreciate this."

I told him it was no problem.

"I can't believe I left the van unlocked. I mean, I see crackies 'round here all the time."

I acknowledged that one had to be careful.

"Don't know why they covered it in chocolate sauce, though."

I said that I didn't either.

I don't know precisely what I was hoping for, but I expected something. Not a reward. I knew that nothing more was coming other than another handshake. I knew that I would never know him any better than I had reading his files. But suddenly, I didn't want this chance convergence to end so quickly. There were bars around the corner. We could grab a drink, I thought, gripe about women. We could go to the strip club together. I felt we had things to learn from each other—I could help him pull things together a little bit; he could show me how to move through life with greater ease.

But instead we just watched the empty street in silence for a long couple of beats, then at last shook hands and returned to our separate lives.

THE FAIRY TREE ON JULIAN AVENUE

Jesse Thorn

Jesse Thorn is the host and producer of the public radio show and podcast *The Sound of Young America*.

I grew up in the eighties, in San Francisco's Mission District. These days, the neighborhood is known for its upscale hipsters and boutique record stores. During the Reagan years, though, it was much more, well, gritty. Neither of my parents had a car, so we spent a lot of time walking, and I spent a lot of time with my eyes to the ground, looking for anything I could pick up and add to one of my collections. At one point, my mother bought me a hardware cabinet to house my "mineral collection," which was largely composed of objects a normal person would call rocks.

It was lucky for my folks—and me—that my collections were as benign as rocks, broken toys, and eucalyptus nuts. It would have been easy, at the age of six, to have started a Bic-pen-turned-crack-pipe collection, or a disease-laced-syringe collection, or maybe a discarded-soiled-condom collection. It was that kind of neighborhood—imagine Sesame Street, only not clean, and with junkies instead of Muppets. This urban milieu was made even more remarkable when we discovered the Fairy Tree, and, by extension, my ray gun collection.

The Fairy Tree was on Julian Avenue, a little residential street off of Sixteenth Street, which was a big thoroughfare for the neighborhood's cholos and punk rockers (there must have been other kinds of people in the neighborhood, but I only remember red-and-white Nike Air Cortezes and black Doc Martens). Julian is a little street and our church was at the end of it. Though it was never the most direct route to anywhere we might want to go, my friends and I often walked along Julian to avoid another street, where kids on the roof of a housing project liked to hurl C-cell batteries at us.

The first thing we found under this tree was a ray gun. I should be clear that this ray gun did not actually shoot deadly space rays, but it was white, plastic, and had a handle and a gunlike shape. No one knew what it was or where it came from, so I made some educated guesses. I guessed that it was a ray gun, and had been placed there by fairies. My neighbor at the time, Gus Iversen, had rich grandparents who'd bought him every single Master of the Universe toy, including vehicles and castles. He'd even accumulated doubles of He-Man and Man-at-Arms, and, oddly, three Prince Adams. But I had a fucking ray gun.

Not long after, we found a hamster cage on Julian Ave. Same tree, same magic. It was a serendipitous find, as my family needed a hamster cage at the time—somehow we had a hamster but no cage. This great, loyal hamster cage served us through many hamsters, including the one my father stepped on, which is a long story for a different book.

A few months later, we found a different ray gun. I'm just going to take a moment to acknowledge the monumental nature of all of this. To recap: First I found a ray gun under a tree, which I then decided was a magic tree. Later, I found a second ray gun. I began, in other words, a *ray gun collection* courtesy of this magic tree. Truly spectacular.

The second ray gun was better, too. It was like the Uzi to the previous ray gun's Saturday Night Special. I still have this thing, and it's still amazing to me. Its handle and business end are both adjustable by turning various cranks, it's got a trigger you can pull, and also these crazy black things that come out and go into these other things, and it's just a fucking delight.

I struggled to understand why fairies were so into ray guns, rather than pixie dust or maybe fairy dew, but that hardly seemed important. What was really important was that I had two ray guns and that fairies had given them to me by way of a Fairy Tree.

Even after I got older and moved from childhood into adolescence, there was no explanation for these devices. I showed them to a lot of people, and a lot of people, flummoxed, agreed that they must be ray guns, given to me by fairies. One day, not too long ago, a doctor friend said she thought it might be a surgical stapler. I have only stapled in an office context, so I decided to stick with ray gun. What does a doctor know about surgical staplers, anyway?

What's special about something that's been found isn't what it is—it's the possibilities it represents. There's only the tiniest sliver of objective truth, and you have the opportunity to fill in the rest however you please. Upon finding something, you get a taste of that sense of possibility that surrounds you when you're six, but leaks away as you get older. By the time you're sixteen or twenty, the world can be distressingly literal. But when you read a scrap of a love note, you get to be six years old, if only for a moment. You can leave the world of observed truth for a vacation in the world of potential truth. That's where a surgical stapler becomes a ray gun.

Or *two* ray guns.

EVERYTHING'S GONNA COME OUT TODAY

Julian Goldberger

Julian Goldberger is the director of the films *Trans* and *The Hawk Is Dying*, starring Paul Giamatti.

My name is Julian Goldberger. The voice mail on my cell phone says, very clearly, "Hello, you've reached Julian Goldberger." And yet, from time to time, I find a message that somebody's left for someone besides Julian Goldberger. One of the weirdest of these came a few years ago when I was still living in Florida:

> Hello . . . This is Samantha Bawks . . . and uh, I'm callin' because, uh . . . I . . . uh . . . Freddie Krane is harassing me . . . and my number is eight three five two eight six eight . . . And um . . . I don't know what for . . . uh, I don't . . . I . . . uh, guess they scared I know too much on 'em . . . Which I do!! But I'm not gonna say nothin' . . . but they won't leave me alone anyway . . . so I might as well tell!! So . . . and uh . . . I'm not gonna sit up here for another four months in terror . . . with a, uh . . . five-hundred-thousand-dollar . . . uh . . . uh . . . accidental . . . uh . . . I mean a death claim on me . . . okay? I want some protection . . . I don't know what's happenin' here . . . I'm callin' lawyers and everything . . . I'm about to lose my mind . . . and I'm sick of it!!

And I don't care . . . I'd rather be dead . . . if I got to live like this . . .
So ask him to call me and help me . . . I already got a lawyer . . .
Everything's gonna come out today!! Thank you.

I listened to the message again and again; I even recorded it and played it for my brother. The more I listened, though, the foggier I grew on how to proceed. Samantha Bawks was desperate for help—wasn't it my obligation to let her know that her call had missed its mark? On the other hand, I had the eerie sense that if I got involved, soon enough Freddie Krane would be coming for me, too. I kept thinking of Kyle MacLachlan in *Blue Velvet*, and the way he'd found a bloody ear in the grass and had followed its trail into a world of grotesque darkness. I mean, I like grotesque darkness as much as the next fellow, but I also like, you know, living.

I never called Samantha Bawks.

FINDING IT, FINDING HIM, FINDING ME

Eldad Malamuth

Eldad Malamuth is a writer and lawyer living in Chicago.

Trusting that you won't break into my house and rob me blind, I'll let you in on my high-tech security system: I hide the valuables in between the pages of books. Any paper that at some point seemed precious, like my passport, the deed to my house, and my Barry Bonds rookie cards, I've tucked away on the bookshelves. "Once in a while," I forget in which specific novel I hid something and I'm forced to go down the rows, flipping the pages until I find what I'm looking for.

Not long ago in a furious search for lost euros, I found in a John Irving classic a photograph, which probably was a bookmark and not a treasure, although I'm not completely sure. In the picture, which I'd taken years ago with a crappy disposable camera, a young man sits underneath a wooden barrow in Jerusalem. His face is mostly hidden because of the shade, but you can make out some features and his mop of curly hair. Looking at the shadowy figure in the three-by-five, I remembered with a rush how good it felt to find him there.

In 1993, I spent the summer after high school graduation in Israel. One hot night in late July, a few friends and I slept on the beach in the resort town of Netanya, on the Mediterranean Sea between Tel Aviv and Haifa. During the night a ne'er-do-well rifled through my friend Sol's stuff, but the night was still rich with the sound of the waves and the open air. Someone took a picture in the morning in which you see a mess of sleeping bodies and camping gear, including my sandals and skinny legs on a bed of light-hued sand.

We collected our backpacks, headed to the bus station, and bought tickets for the next ride to Jerusalem. Because we had extra time, we traded shifts waiting with the packs and walking around the stores down the street. The summer temperature in Israel varies between dangerously hot and deathly, and I went to buy a carbonated apple juice—never underestimate the refreshing power of carbonated apple juice. About ten minutes before the scheduled departure time, I came back to find that where my friends had once been was now an empty space. Our packs were missing, too.

All I had were my shorts, T-shirt, and sandals, and in my pockets were my passport, a disposable camera, and about a hundred shekels. This was long before the days of cell phones, e-mail, electronic tickets, and all the miracles that make modern travel so effortless. So I had to guess how and why I'd been left alone in a foreign country with little money. Three scenarios seemed possible: (1) the bus had left early and my friends were on it, (2) my friends were playing a practical joke on me and hiding somewhere nearby, and (3) my friends had ditched me for good. I decided to hop on the next bus to Jerusalem, hoping I'd reconnect with them there.

The bus wound its way through the Judean foothills and I squinted at the sun-baked terrain and took in its rugged, cracked beauty. I remembered that my friend's older sister had died on a similar bus ride a few years earlier when a terrorist grabbed the wheel and forced the vehicle into a deep gorge. The memory was unsettling, but it also made me realize that my current predicament was not—in the scheme of things—such a big deal.

Near Jerusalem, the bus driver announced a further twist. A bomb threat had forced the evacuation of the bus station. The bus stopped a few blocks away from its original destination, and I realized with some concern that I couldn't reach the one place that my friends would know to wait for me, if in fact they were waiting for me.

Later, my friends told me what had happened in Netanya—the bus had arrived and they'd loaded our packs onboard and waited. When the bus started to leave early, my friend Steven went up the aisle and began to explain to the bus driver that I wasn't there yet.

"I have a friend—" Steven began saying.

"I have a friend, too," the bus driver said, and drove away. The bus drivers in Israel held inexplicable power and wielded it with abandon; apparently the Egged company had a monopoly and the drivers had an excellent union. On an earlier stop in Tel Aviv, we had boarded a bus and Steven had asked the bus driver, who was wearing torn jeans and blasting Metallica, "Could you tell me if—" but he'd used the wrong "to tell" verb, choosing one that denoted narration instead of explanation. "I'll tell you a story," the bus driver had said as he closed the door and pulled away.

At the time, however, I had no idea what happened at the Netanya bus station or where my friends were. All I knew was that it was so hot and bright I could practically see through my eyelids. If it came to it, I thought, I could always throw myself at the mercy of some orthodox group in the Old City that would provide me shelter in exchange for some temporary piety. In the meantime, my vague plan was to walk down Jaffa Road and see if a better strategy came to mind. Miraculously, my plan worked.

Sometimes in the Israeli summer you have to find whatever shade you can. Before my search passed the five-minute mark, I thought I'd spotted a familiar profile in an unfamiliar spot—as I approached, I saw that, indeed, it was my friend Cal, who'd taken refuge from the sun on the ground beneath an orange juice cart. That's when I snapped the picture of him, happy to chronicle this providence. Cal told me that my friends had fanned out to different spots around the bus station to look for me, which meant it wasn't serendipity that had reunited us so much as their sensible plan, but still, I was glowing to be back in their company.

Sometimes, finding someone isn't about knowing where to look, it's about having the right people to look for. I've always felt blessed that way.

And sometimes, the best way of finding things is to have a terrible filing system.

Mike Schank

Mike Schank, featured in the documentary *American Movie*, lives in Milwaukee, Wisconsin, with his wife, Kate. He plays guitar and has won almost four thousand dollars playing scratch-off lottery tickets.

In real life, I never find anything too interesting, just losing scratch tickets, which I finish scratching off to make sure they're not winners, and cigarette butts, which I smoke. But I do find notes all the time in my dreams.

Some people think dreams are reality. I have dreams where I'm on other planets like Mars and Venus and hanging out all around me there's these supersmart gorillas that have a bunch of eyes. There's always papers blowing every which way and lots more crumpled on the ground by my feet. I like to pick them up and read them. Last night, I found one note that just said, "I DON'T KNOW," and another note that said, "HAVE A MIND OF YOUR OWN, IMAGINE." They're just as confusing as fortune cookie fortunes, but fifty times as big. I think you have to be a gorilla with a ton of eyes to understand what they really mean.

Next to my bed, I keep a box of fan letters, and sometimes I like to read through them before I go to sleep. Maybe having that stack of pages there is why I find so many notes blowing around in my dreams. I can't help but pick up every one of them. See, you've got to understand, dreams are my reality.

THE OLD CLERK'S DIARY

Katherine Dunn

Katherine Dunn is the author of the novels *Geek Love*, *Attic*, and *Truck*. Her latest book is called *The Cut Man*.

I n my apartment building, in the lobby, there's a "free" pile. Anyone in the building can contribute things, as long as they're still usable. Visit the lobby anytime and you'll find things of value: books, ornaments, kitchen appliances, furniture, the strange or ridiculous—it's all there; the pile's an amazement. I love the thrill of finding something unexpected.

The same is true of furniture that's been left out on the curb. I'd always rather have a chair from the street, with its own life and history—stories you can't know but can speculate about—than one purchased new at Ikea. By the same token, I don't go around reading other people's mail, but I'm definitely an eavesdropper. Eavesdropping is a kind of found conversation, full of revelations of people's interior lives. That's why I love people on cell phones—they may irritate others, but to me they're a treasure chest of overheard dialogue.

Once, in a building that I used to live in, I was helping the building manager clean out the apartment of an elderly woman who'd lived there for many, many years and had recently died, and late in the day, I discovered the old woman's diary. When I opened it to the first page, I was immediately hooked.

The woman had a led a simple life of sorts—she was a clerk at a department store for forty years and had never married—but I was captivated by the tiny ups and downs of her solitary life. Most of the entries were very short, just a few sentences—she'd talk about a trip to the dentist's office or getting off early from work—while others spanned several pages. In her meticulous handwriting, she'd record the fleeting interactions she'd have with men she was interested in. She'd compliment them in the most discreet and ladylike fashion, then always return home alone to her cozy little apartment and have her sister over for a game of cribbage. In a way, it was a very limited and sad life that she'd led, but in her journal she never seemed upset by her solitude. I think that there were times in her life when she'd felt deeply lonely, but mostly it seemed that in the last forty or fifty years of her life she'd found a way to be alone but not lonely. She reached out to friends from time to time and really enjoyed their company, but didn't appear to grieve or feel a great hole in her life when she was alone. Ultimately, she seemed remarkably content.

Loneliness, I've come to believe, is largely the domain of the young. When you're young, you're so dependent on contact with peers, their constant acknowledgment; you need them around to process meaning out of your daily life. There's a sharpness to being alone that rounds and softens as you age.

I still think about that old woman sometimes. Her journal was like a relic from another time, though she'd lived into modern times. I never learned her name—it's mentioned nowhere in her diary. It may seem strange, but I felt no compunction whatsoever in keeping her journal and reading it. She had no family; this thing was bound for the trash. I actually felt like I was doing her a kind of justice by reading her life story, and I think she would've been happy to know how much it affected me.

There are so many different kinds of lives being led. When you read a journal like this old woman's journal, and you peer so deeply into a stranger's life, it expands your imagination so that you can't look at other people—a woman on the bus, a guy on a park bench—without wondering about them and what their lives might be like. You feel a sense of communion with the people you share the world with—it's a way of connecting with the cosmic consciousness.

Poetry works its magic in a similar way. It's often been composed by someone in a far-off place who's now long gone, but somehow it reaches across time, across culture, even across language, and touches other people. To me, found letters and notes, like the old clerk's diary, are the poetry of the universe.

Jim Carroll

Jim Carroll is a poet, autobiographer, punk musician, and the author of eight books, including *The Basketball Diaries*. He lives in New York City.

Back in the day when I was playing rock and roll and touring a lot, we had this roadie from the Bay Area named Dennis. Dennis had a girlfriend in the Bay and she had a friend who I'd get together with when I was in town. One time, me and Dennis took his girlfriend and her friend to a spa. They kept saying they wanted to go to one, so we finally went and they did their thing while me and Dennis sat around looking at the clouds.

Then we happened to notice that one of the things they offered at this spa was colonics. This is the service where they pump water up your ass and you shit all this stuff out; the idea is that it's cleansing for the body and the soul. It was expensive, maybe a hundred bucks, and I knew Dennis was short on cash,

D. T.

but we were there and it seemed like the thing to do, so I threw down the money for both of us.

Once they've pumped the water into you, you let it all out over a fine-mesh screen, a net of sorts, so all the liquid goes through and what's left on the screen is whatever was inside you. The colonics experts don rubber gloves and sift through the debris and analyze it all—this is stuff from your lower bowel that you usually wouldn't be shitting out; it's the shit that collects in you over time.

It was disgusting. The guy held up a piece of pork that he guessed had been in my system for three years. I couldn't have been more grossed out or more fucking fascinated. Me and Dennis kept marveling at the whole notion that things could stay in your body for so long.

But here's the real killer of the thing: You know those little green plastic soldiers you can get a bag of for ninety-nine cents at the general store? Every kid has them. They come in different positions—one guy is a sniper on the ground, another is kneeling; there's also the officer with a pistol, the guy with binoculars, one guy with a machine gun, one with a bazooka. I used to play with them endlessly when I was a kid, whether I was outdoors or inside, creating little battlefields. All the kids I knew had a similar collection of army guys. And invariably, someone would bite the head off of one of them by accident and start chewing on it like they were chewing on anything, so every once in a while, naturally, you'd hear that so-and-so had swallowed one of the heads.

Well, at some point in his childhood, Dennis must have swallowed an army guy whole, because that day at the spa while he was getting his colonic treatment, an entire U.S. soldier came out of his ass. We found it caught in his screen after he'd cleared out his insides. We couldn't even tell what it was at first, but once they'd washed it off, we saw that it was a full-on plastic soldier—one of my favorites, actually—the sniper shimmying along on his belly. It must have been inside him for over twenty years.

The most amazing thing about the whole scene, it seemed to me, was the way it redefined the phrase "You are what you eat." Dennis was always a nice, quiet guy, but he got real fucking rowdy when he drank. He got up in people's faces; he got in fights. Now it made sense—he'd had a soldier inside of him since the age of six.

The colonics guys at the spa were flabbergasted—they said they'd never seen anything like this before. They'd found talons, bones, and marbles, but never a plastic soldier. And Dennis seemed to grow mellower once that soldier was out of him. I've always loved picking up interesting stuff—letters, pictures, old books in an alley—but that soldier, sopped with goop, caught in the mesh screen and trying to wriggle away while keeping his rifle steady, was one of the best things I've ever found.

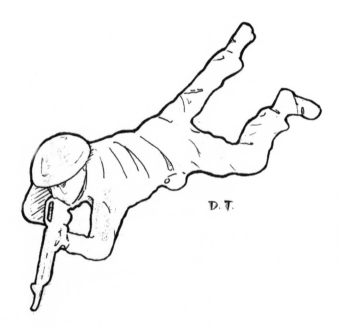

D. T.

GOOD TIMES

Damon Wayans

Damon Wayans is a stand-up comedian, writer, and actor from New York City.

I'll tell you what I found—comedy. This is the story of how I found comedy: my career, my best friend.

I first got into stand-up when I was twenty-two. My brother Keenan was already a comedian. He was like a god to me—I kept telling my wife how amazing he was. I talked about him so much that she told me if I didn't get out there myself and go up onstage, she was going to leave me and marry Keenan.

My first time onstage was at this club called Good Times, which was in Manhattan at Third Avenue and Thirty-first Street, and is probably closed now. I deliberately went alone to a place where I knew I'd know no one. I knew that if I performed in front of people I knew, I would never do it again, and I would feel like I'd let them down. Comedy is such a personal thing—you have to find the warrior within yourself. If you're looking for approval from people you already know, chances are they're gonna say, "Man, you should go back to your day job, it's not worth it." Very few people understand your passion, your dream, and how you can work at it and get better.

It was the middle of winter, and I went up onstage wearing a big, heavy leather jacket. I'd written down my jokes on a piece of paper and had it in my jacket pocket to refer to during my set, but I got so hot so fast once I was onstage that I took it off and threw it into the crowd. Then I was like, *Holy shit— all my jokes are gone!* I started off with this one: "I'm from a poor family; we're so poor my father drives a 1974 Big Wheel." After that, I was improvising. I wish I still had that page with the set I'd written for that first night—and I wish I still had that leather jacket.

It was amazing, though, the best feeling ever, because besides that one joke, I was totally unrehearsed. I was probably onstage for about seven minutes, but it felt like forever. After I walked off the stage, all I remembered was the laughter—not the six and a half minutes of silence, but the thirty seconds of laughter. That's the drug. I felt like I had a giant woody. People might've been clapping me on the shoulder, telling me I did a good job, but I was so full of adrenaline that their words just sounded like Charlie Brown's teachers. It's a magical experience to think of something, and you think it's funny, and then you share it with a room full of people, and they think it's funny, too. And you realize it's not just one time that you can do it—you can go to this club and get a laugh, go to that club and get a laugh. You become a laugh junkie. It was the greatest high ever. I walked over to the west side of Manhattan to catch the subway, and on the train home, I replayed my whole time onstage in my mind in slow motion, already thinking about things I could do the next time to make my act better.

That's when I found comedy—it's where my understanding of stand-up came from: It's not what's on the page, it's what's on the stage. Performance is everything.

That night, I ran inside my house and impregnated my wife. And then I just started writing. I did my next show immediately after the first. Once you're hooked, you're hooked for life.

How I Spent My Summer Vacation

Jenny Owen Youngs

Jenny Owen Youngs is a singer/songwriter based in New York City. Her debut album is called _Batten Down the Hatches._

By the time I got to Cleveland, I had been touring solo through the Midwest for about a week. Although the audiences had been lovely and the cities fair, driving across American turnpikes all alone had left me feeling pretty drained. I had also earned a general _blerg_ feeling by indulging in every local delicacy that came my way (this mostly meant the head-sized German wheat beers of the Indy Biergarten and a boatload of truck-stop food). My behavior, too, was growing loopier. Desperate for companionship, I had laid my lonely heart at the feet of mainstream country radio. I was rewarded with Brad Paisley asserting his masculinity (even if he did walk my sissy dog) and Miranda Lambert preparing to beat her freshly paroled, abusive husband to the proverbial punch by pumping his unsuspecting face full of lead. Somewhere along the line I took to calling out, "Baggins! Shire!" every time I drove past a reasonably attractive bunch of trees. I was totally batty and couldn't wait to get back to Brooklyn. I just had to get through this final night in C-town and then I could head home.

The gig in Cleveland ended up an example of the niche phenomenon I've come to think of as the "sleeper show": that is, one performs before a reserved, seemingly indifferent audience for the length of the set, only to be approached at the merch table by tons of rowdy, enthusiastic people—members, inexplicably, of the same group that seemed to be just barely staying awake for the last hour. The psychological result of playing this kind of show is akin to receiving intensely mixed messages from the sociopath with whom you didn't mean to fall in love. And so, with my brain all swirly and my morale flagging, I rolled wearily out of the venue parking lot toward the hotel around midnight, brain churning out my goal-mantra like so: *bed bed bed bed bed bed bed.*

Cleveland, however, did not want me to sleep.

First I needed to park in front of the hotel lobby. My GPS robot was able to bring me within rock-throwing distance of the hotel, but no closer; multiple orbits revealed that all four roads squaring off the block were under construction. The only way to pull into the hotel's loading area required me to spin diagonally into the intersection, brake, and then back up straight for about half a block, weaving between striped cylindrical barricades all the way. Once parked, I approached reception to check in. The clerk's marginal interest in me completely disintegrated when a coworker emerged from a conference room with a steel cart full of untouched catering leftovers. He abandoned ship mid-transaction, leaving the desk to make up a plate of food and forgetting to give me my room number. Eventually he came back and told me where to sleep. I stashed my gear in the room and hopped back into my car to look for parking. Mr. GPS listed about ten parking garages within a mile of the hotel. When I drove to the closest one, however, I was greeted by a locked gate and a sign that read OPEN 6AM–12AM—NO OVERNIGHT PARKING. Further investigation revealed that every other garage in the area operated by the same hours. I finally settled on what appeared to be street parking, albeit ambiguously signed, and then fell into the bed at around one-thirty.

The following morning I rose at six, anxious to start heading eastward. I darted into Starbucks to feed my caffeine addiction. I'm not a huge fan of their coffee, but it is the one place I can rely on to have soy milk anywhere in America. Except, I quickly learned, Cleveland. I began to unhinge. *This city hates me,* I thought. I was exhausted, homesick, and now there was no soy milk. Hulk smash, damn it!! Throat tightening in the premenstrual manifestation of anger (read: tears), I stalked across the street to my car with my black coffee, and that's when I saw it. Tucked under my windshield wiper just so lay a peace offering—though I didn't know it yet—from the city to me. Figuring it was a coupon for a car wash or a tiny flyer for a rave, I picked it up and read:

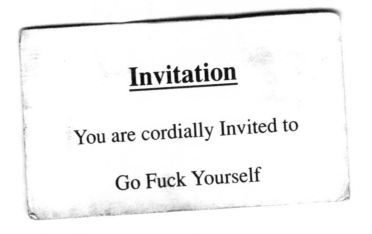

I broke into uncontrollable laughter, as I turned the business card over in my hands, wondering who would have such a thing printed up, and who would walk around Cleveland between the hours of one and six in the morning, Johnny Appleseed–ing tidings of "Get fucked." I inspected the other two cars parked on the block, but the angel of death passed over all but me.

The effect the card had on me, though, was perhaps the reverse of what was intended: I felt a strange smile creep over my face. Finally, I hopped in my car, started it, and took off toward the rising sun, toward home.

THE FRANKENSTEIN CAR

Chuck D

Chuck D is a rapper, author, and activist and founder of the rap group Public Enemy.

As a kid, I had a thing for old coins. I'd walk around my neighborhood looking down, looking for old pennies and subway tokens. I was fascinated by it all—screws, bolts, little springs and other things that popped off of trucks and cars, toys, paper clips, paper bits, broken bits of jewelry. I collected all of it.

Later on, when I got into music, I discovered that just about any piece of equipment I needed I could find on the street. It amazed me what people would put out on the curb. I was that rare cat who raced around the neighborhood just ahead of the garbage trucks, filling my car with stuff. Microphone stands. Amps. Old radios. Old turntables. I'd find a busted speaker and tinker with it for a few hours until I got it working again. All of my early gear was just other people's junk, headed for the dump.

Then I fell in love with auto junkyards. Other guys were showing off their brand-new rides; I was always reconstructing a car out of pieces. Mine was the Frankenstein car, a yellow '69 Malibu with a black door, a red door, and green spackling all across the back. Then I upgraded to a baby blue '68 LeMans. I made do with parts I turned up in junkyards. Once, on my way home from my job at Sears, the LeMans was battling a transmission leak. I saw some fresh pavement that had just been laid down, still baking in the afternoon sun, so I pulled over, scraped up a bit of tar with a stick, and dabbed it on the leak to plug the hole. It held for four weeks.

My favorite junkyard was out on Long Island, a field of broken glass and old rubber tires. I'd dig for hours, not even sure what I was looking for, until that moment when I saw a beautiful front grille, or a gleaming side mirror with a nice cut to it. The feeling when I found the perfect part for my car was exquisite. I was harvesting gemstones in a sea of wreckage.

To this day, I'm always looking on the ground, checking out piles of junk on the corner. As a society, we put so much emphasis on new, new, new, new, but I'd always rather find something I need than go to a store and buy it. Your trash? That's my treasure.

MAD GRATITUDE

This book wouldn't be in your hands without the unbelievable hard work, energy, kindness, generosity, and devotion of the following people:

Sarah Locke.
James Molenda.
Michelle Quint.
Jason Bitner.
Amanda Patten.
Jud Laghi.

Brande Wix, Todd Doty, Jordan Miller, Chris Loud,
Kimberly Chou, and Gino Sorcinelli.

Trish Todd, Mark Gompertz, Lauren Spiegel, Marcia Burch, Kelly Bowen,
Tricia Wygal, Mary Austin Speaker, Richard Oriolo,
Cherlynne Li, and Amber Husbands.

Andrew Cohn, Jacob van Putten, Lauren Hall, Eli Horowitz, Angela Petrella,
Chris Ying, Andrew Leland, Dave Eggers, Peter Rothbart, Frank Warren,
Richie Kern, Larry Sanitsky, Elwood Reid, Nancy Josephson, Tim McIlrath,
Robb Bindler, Matthew Bass, Anna Stothard, Will Reiser, Margaret Box,
Brett Loudermilk, Stephen Colbert, Drew Barrymore, Chelsie O'Donnell,
Betsy Lerner, Nicole Aragi, Sarah McIntire, Andrea Troolin, NowOn, Pete Smolin,
Chris Wallace, Josh Evans, Evelyn Case, Sylvia McClellan, Kate Schank,
Roger Bennett, Jolyn Matsumuro, Yvette Shearer, Dani Davis,
Al McWilliams, and Mark Winegardner.

'Nuff respect due to Dan Tice, Brendt Rioux, Ben Snakepit, and Ghostshrimp
for their imaginative illustrations, completed—literally—under the gun (okay,
it was a BB gun). And to Michael Wartella for his colorful cover art.

All kinds of love to everyone who has supported *FOUND* over the years—
bookstores, media folks, magazine subscribers, tour friends,
and especially the finders!

My eternal gratitude—and drinks on me next time I see you—to each of
the brilliant, beautifully demented artists and prose marksmen who
contributed pieces for this collection. You guys fucking rock!

And finally, well, goddamn—thank *you* for reading.
PEACE—DAVY

ABOUT THE EDITOR

Davy Rothbart is the creator of *Found* magazine, editor of the bestselling *Found* books, a frequent contributor to public radio's *This American Life*, and author of the story collection *The Lone Surfer of Montana, Kansas*. He writes regularly for *GQ*, and his work has been featured in *The New Yorker*, *The New York Times*, and *High Times*. Rothbart is also the subject of the upcoming documentary *My Heart Is an Idiot*. He lives in Ann Arbor, Michigan.

Much like the lost, tossed, and forgotten items in the *Found* books, Davy's stories capture the oddity, poetry, and dignity of everyday life.

"Davy writes with his whole heart. These stories are crushing."
—ARTHUR MILLER

THE LONE SURFER OF MONTANA, KANSAS

STORIES

DAVY ROTHBART
AUTHOR OF THE NATIONAL BESTSELLER
FOUND